**Luis Carrasco** lives and writes in Gloucestershire. He was inspired to write *El Hacho* after falling in love with the people and natural beauty of the Sierra de Grazalema whilst living in Andalucía. He is currently working on his second novel.

*Luis Carrasco*

# El Hacho

époque press

Published by Epoque Press in 2018
www.epoquepress.com



Typeset in Dante MT by Palimpsest Book Production Ltd, Falkirk, Stirlingshire
Printed and bound in Great Britain by Clays Ltd, St Ives plc

British Library Cataloguing-in-Publication Data
A catalogue record for this book is available from the British Library

ISBN 978-1-9998960-0-3 (Paperback edition)
ISBN 978-1-9998960-1-0 (Electronic edition)

*For my mother*

# El Hacho

# *One*

The first time the man came up from Málaga the boy stood only as high as his father's belt loops and he leaned into them and listened as the Malagueño made his pitch.

His father listened respectfully whilst the offer was laid out before them and nodded his head and listened and nodded some more. When all was said his father apologised to the Malagueño for having made such a long journey for no reward. He pressed a litter of stove-warm almonds into his visitor's hand and closed his fingers around them and left the offer unanswered.

When the Malagueño returned a week later to ask again, the boy was brushed off the porch by his father so he could talk to the man alone but he only went as far as the figs and twisted his head through the weave of silver branches and strained his neck to listen.

His father was a man for whom actions carried more

weight than words so after a while he raised a palm to halt the speech he'd heard a week before and cupped the Malagueño's elbow to lead him to the edge of the terrace. He pointed to the north and the curve of olives that ringed El Hacho's base.

Would you ask a butcher to sell his block, he said, or a carpenter his plane and chisel? Without those trees I'm just a man, which isn't much to be.

You think the price not fair? the Malagueño said. With what we offer you can buy ten times this many.

That so, but where would I plant them where I can work more happily than this?

The Malagueño frowned and cast his eyes around. This land is steep and filled with rocks, he said. What pleasure can it bring to work so hard amongst it when our offer can free you to farm a gentler pasture or not to farm at all? The mountain is worth more to us in stone than it could ever yield to you in fruit. This offer is a lot of money to dismiss without thinking what it can buy. Consider it a while at least.

The boy's father filled his chest and breathed out slowly and locked his fingers behind his head. Then he glossed his hand over the valley to the south-east, over the pink lace of the almond blossom, over the white toe of the Montejaque village and beyond to where the land buckled in a granite ribbon. The dipping sun crept around El Hacho's flank and fired the valley slopes with a copper glaze.

And what could I buy with ten times your offer that could give me more than this?

Finally the Malagueño gave him the respect of his silence and dropped his head in defeat. His host led him off the terrace and told him not to come again unless it was to share a cup of wine and not to talk of money.

I'll lie under the shadow of this mountain, he said, when it's my time, and feed these trees with my body. There is no other way. Go with God on the road back to Málaga and seek your stone elsewhere.

When he remounted the terrace he ran his fingers upon the boy's face to push the hair from his eyes and kissed his forehead.

Get your brother from his mischief, he said. Then we can eat.

# *Two*

Curro stared down the bull for longer than he was accustomed, and read the sadness in its eyes.

How many times, he said, do we have to go through this? How many new ways can you find to break in here? If they'd ever put you in the corrida you would have charmed your way back out and kept your balls for sure. Come on you brute, let's do it easy and save yourself the stick.

It was an empty threat. Curro never used the stick to flush it out. He knew it wouldn't make it move any faster. He knew because he watched his neighbour, Jesus, thrash the hide from the bull's bones when he was picking asparagus from beneath the scree on El Hacho's southern edge. Jesus beat it for sport and hacked out great clods of its filthy coat, but the bull would not give him the satisfaction of knowing that it felt the blows, nor would it charge him down. Its spirit was as broken as the walls of its owner's cortijo and its knees trembled with age under the weight of its shoulders but its hunger always led it to Curro's olives and the grasses that swayed beneath them.

Out! Curro cried and clapped his hands and whipped his arms around him. He clapped some more and stamped his boots as hard as the borrachos at the Goyesca in September, when the carnival lights the night with fireworks and wine, but the bull would only blink its eyes and mist the air around its muzzle in the cool blue evening light.

Out! he shouted again. You have to go, and when you do you can watch me fix another fence for you to break. He slapped his palms and wrung his throat until it parched and kicked at the fragile dust beneath his boots. The bull let him tire and when he did, it lifted its hooves to turn and showed the blood red welts across its hollow back.

Soon a slender hand slipped through Curro's and another cupped it from the front to hold it in a bundle.

How does he do it? she asked and put a cheek upon his arm.

He comes to test my faith in God, Curro sighed, so He must show him how.

You think it's the food or your performance he comes for?

The food, but he never leaves before I'm done.

How about some for you?

What is it?

Rabbit.

I need to see him out.

He'll go, she said. Let's eat.

They turned to walk towards the house and lifted their feet to clear the roots from which the wind had gouged the soil and he steadied her with an outstretched arm until they made the terrace and the pool of light that lay there. As he eased his ankle from a boot with the toe of the other he stopped and stood full in the doorway.

What day is it? he asked.

Sunday, why?

I didn't change the flowers up there.

I don't know why you bother, she said. Your father always said the place for flowers is in the ground, not drying up on gravestones.

I don't do it for him.

I know.

Remind me tomorrow, before Marie comes up.

I will, she said. But come on in now, the sauce is sticking.

He paired his boots beside the mat and latched the door and put the terrace light out.

# Three

The sun was early on the terrace and made its heat upon it before the cockerel came. Curro lapped the coffee grounds against his cup and set it down and pushed against the shutter to light the kitchen. Then he washed the cup and ran his hand across his chin to dwell upon another day of unremitting heat.

It has to break, he thought. The land demands it does and he tried again in vain to remember a time in which the rain had been so long in coming. He fastened his sleeves back to his elbows and shucked off his slippers beneath the stove then sawed an edge of bread and took it with his boots across the terrace to the steps where he sat and ate and pulled them on. He eyed the angle of the sun and judged its warmth. He still had time to water the herbs and flowers that glistened with a filmy dew before the angel of life and death reared implacably above the valley wall and scorched the thin leaves dry.

He thrust the can deep into the tub and heaved it full and spread the water around the borders of the vegetable patch. Then he wet the row of claywork pots sitting against the wall beneath the windows and then the ones that begged a little shade around the side of the house and up the slope towards the olives. When the can was dry he pulled at a few weeds that had found a shallow footing amongst the stunted crops and shook his head in pity at them, both crops and weeds. He pushed his thumb into a pepper and clucked his tongue because the flesh was soft and wilting and then announced that nothing much would come to his table from this patch until the rain would let it. He stepped back upon the terrace and pinched a fist of pink-lipped flowers from a claywork pot and a sprig of lavender from the border and scuffed his heels along the track which headed away from the house towards El Hacho's sun-bleached belly and his parents' grave.

He eased his knees down to the stone and placed the flowers in the dust beside it and scratched around his ears. Then he took the withered strands that fell around the sides of the glass jar atop the tomb and lay them next to the fresh ones and swirled the stagnant water out onto the ground and reached behind the headstone to lift the wooden plug of the cask he'd buried full of water from the stream. He groped at the ladle inside and filled the jar sparingly. Then he arranged the new flowers in a clumsy manner and laid the lavender at the foot of the jar and replaced the wooden lid of the cask. His ritual complete he spoke to his father.

I know what you're thinking Papa.

You are telling me it is a waste of both flowers and water. Especially the water, when the land sobs so deeply for its absence but what should I lay here, a handful of dust? A little monument of olive pits? How do I find your approval for this thing we do, this thing we have always done? We honour our dead in the shadow of this great rock but its shadow, its weight falls heaviest upon those still working beneath it.

How is it that I never heard you complain? Even when Mama was taken from us you still had a calmness, a manner to make us all understand that this is simply the way things are. I remember us all sitting around the fire after we buried her, with the embers flaring in the grate and Jose-Marie crying like a child and the sadness and anger seeping through the room and you, implacable, like a god, you took him in your arms like you did when he was a child with a bloody knee and told him to only ever think of her with joy in his heart. You said that it's better to light a candle than complain about the darkness, so why do I fear so much for the future of this land? Why can't I realise your faith?

I've never seen it this bad Papa. So dry and wasted. So pained. But sitting here in front of you I know I don't have the right to complain. I know *you* wouldn't. This is why I bring the flowers still. This is my candle.

His reverence done, Curro lifted his head and rested a palm on the warm grey stone and stroked the length of it and fingered a nail into the inscription to remove the patina of powdery lichen and then pushed himself to his feet. He crossed the track where the bull had hoofed a corrugated lattice in the earth and pulled some fruit from the tree and rolled it in his fingers. A pair of choughs split from the tree and whirled around him and fled to sanctuary on the higher slopes and chattered there upon it. The olives baubled all around him but their number never was a worry to him. He always let a fifth of what came through fall to the ground at harvest just to nourish the year to come as his father had showed him how, so he never feared for the tree's fecundity.

What troubled him now was the fruit itself. Without the rain it had failed to flesh and the skin creased a little like his own dry fingertips and the olives hung weakly on their stalks, unresponsive to the touch and sad like rickety children. He pressed at one with his thumb and narrowed his eyes as it leaked a joyless strand of juice that barely made it to his wrist. The year before they'd burst like larks at roost.

He sucked at the juice and rubbed the flesh into his teeth and spat against the trunk and made his way back down the track. As he came upon the stable block he used for storing tools he heard the car upon the drive and so continued on towards it. It circled on the gravel and then stopped. Jose-Marie clambered out and started towards the house but caught Curro approaching from the stable and walked towards him. He dragged his canvas satchel behind him like a dog, dredging the dust and clattering around his boots.

Sounds like she needs a little oil, Curro said.

You have some?

Not for cars.

Then she'll carry on needing. Has Carmen finished with the coffee? Marie said, as he pushed his finger up under his nose and pointed it at the house.

She went to the village for flour but the stove should still be up. The pot will need clearing. Get us both some.

Marie scowled and kicked back down the track. Curro watched his brother go into the house and checked his watch and wound it round and flicked at the dial with his nail and turned upon the track. The sun was heavy on his neck and as he came upon the stable door a frilly breeze eased up the valley and made him turn in the hope that it bought some clouds on its tail but it did not. The mountains to the sea pierced the cobalt blue above and the breeze died with his hopes.

Inside the stable it was dark and cool and he moved blindly to find the rolls of net lying in bundles against the far wall. He scooped them up and folded them around to save himself another trip and took them down towards the house. He set them on the terrace where he rolled them out in separate squares but found there wasn't room so he took the largest in his hands and kicked the others up against the house and laid the one down flat. Across the net were frayed craters where the nylon had burst at last year's harvest and he reasoned that they wouldn't see another after this one. He returned to the stable and pushed his hands around the shelves until he found the twine and brought it back to the terrace.

His brother handed him the coffee and Curro stood on the lip of the terrace and sucked at it carefully. Marie sat on his haunches and rolled a cigarette with some thin black papers and flicked open a tinder lighter and eased back on his elbows across the coarse brown grass.

Jose-Marie's legs were long and thin about the ankles and his bandy frame bought Curro back to their father's own in its shape and gait when he walked, but there was nothing more in him to recommend the comparison. Marie worked the farm simply because it was what he had to work and he worked it like a weight upon him and not because there was something of him in the soil that made him work it so. Perhaps it was because he was the younger one and had never felt the hereditary pressure that hung over Curro, had never known the responsibility inherent in the line. Or maybe it was because his eye was forever scanning the horizon when their father was set to drilling the mores of the land into their skin. To Ronda, Málaga. Who knew? Maybe even Madrid. Farther than the shadow of El Hacho anyhow.

Regardless, Marie's motivation to up and sweat was always external to himself and more times than not reliant on the example, if not the word of Curro himself. Many times before, Curro thought he should have urged his brother off towards the lights caught in his eyes to see if he would have returned a different man or maybe not at all. There was something uncertain enough in both eventualities to stay his hand until a time came along when he could think it through more clearly.

Soon his wife came up from the almond bank bowed under the weight of a string sack of flour bags, dusting the stone steps as it bounced upon them. She passed over the terrace into the house without a word and came back out without the sack and flexed her knees to collect the cups but took a cushion upon Marie's shoulder as she did and asked him of his wife and young.

The same, he said.

Be thankful of it, she said and caused him a smile. She passed the cups to one hand and pressed the heel of the other against her brow and blew and looked at the nets on the terrace and then gravely at her husband. This heat, the gesture said, will not abate before you start, so pick yourself up before you lose the will.

You are my will, he smiled to her and took another button down on the neck of his shirt and spat into his palms and rubbed them lightly and reached for the ball of twine between his feet and eased himself afoot. He drew a knife from his trouser pocket and set to cutting lengths that dropped onto the net. After cutting ten he stopped and hinged the knife and lowered a knee upon the net and placed the knife beside him and took a strand of twine and sucked at the end. He tied the moistened end to an eye around a puckered hole in the net and began to thread the twine around the perimeter of the hole until he had a true and close circumference. Then he pulled at the twine and watched it draw tight and when it did he looped it around his fingers where they held the net. Then he tied the knot.

He tested it for strength and grunted his satisfaction and moved on to the next crater. His brother rolled another cigarette and grumbled about the heat.

Take the next one, Curro said and brushed a hand towards the rolls of net beneath the window. And start to work this twine. He pulled himself a length as long as the span of his arms and struggled to bite it off and when he did he rifled the ball at his brother's chest.

Go on now.

Marie caught it with both hands and fell back across the grass and lay there, clutching the twine to his chest and blinking at the ocean of blue that lay above, suffocating and pressing them to the land. Then he rose and removed his cloth cap by its peak and wiped the sweat from his brow with his sleeve and replaced the cap. He crossed the terrace and dragged a net back to the grass. By the time Marie had cut his lengths Curro had laced four holes and was working on a fifth.

There are too many holes in these old nets, Marie said. Seems like a lot of trouble to patch them all.

Easier than collecting the fruit that falls through them.

Agreed. But can we not just get some more from Esteban?

We could, Curro smiled.

Why aren't we?

You think you can arrange the credit?

You could.

He'll no sooner give it to me than you.

He knows you'll pay.

It's not a matter of trust, said Curro. Esteban is not a foolish man. If he gives it to me, he'll have every farmer in the Serranía knocking at his door. Then he has to insult people by refusing what he's given to others.

Only if you tell.

You understand the principle though. It's the principle that would stop him. I'd do the same. So would you.

Maybe, said Marie evenly as he knelt low to his net to thread the twine. Actually, I wouldn't. I'd just double the price for credit.

Curro shook his head doubtfully. Double the price for credit, he said.

That's right.

You'd lose friends as fast as you made money.

I'd live with it.

I don't doubt it. Pass me back up the knife.

Curro took the knife and rolled the finished net and laid it on the path and took another from beneath the kitchen window and spread it out and counted the holes. There were only three but one looked too great to tie and he knew he'd have to darn it. That or lose the net. As he cut his lengths he studied his brother from beneath the rim of his hat and saw him working slowly, mechanically, with his mind whirring off someplace else, calculating credit arithmetic or perhaps just thinking of his lunch.

They worked in silence with their backs to the sun and the sweat pooled beneath their knees and their arms and ran in rivulets down the valley of their aching spines. The shadows twisted slowly around the claywork pots and by the time the final net was rolled and stacked upon the path it was time to eat.

Marie slumped against the house and loosened his boots and found his tobacco and laid it down beside him and stared at the high slopes across the valley. The sun was off him now but his forehead glistened still. Curro came from the house with a wooden plate in one hand and a calfskin puron in the other. Marie retrieved his satchel from beneath the window and sat beside him.

Marie took the calfskin puron, uncapped it and gently squeezed a violet jet of wine into his mouth and groaned softly as he drank. Then he opened his satchel and took his bocadillo and untwisted the paper wrapping and folded it carefully back into the bag. He fiddled with the wafers of meat until he had them arrayed exactly as he wished and closed it back up and set upon it wolfishly, stopping only once to chase the food through his dust clogged throat with another splash of wine.

Curro moved through his plate of bread, cheese and oil more slowly and chewed with reverential care. Only when the plate was clear did he siphon the calfskin puron. He passed it back over to his brother and cracked his knuckles and slimmed his eyes.

A symphony of tinny bells hoved into range beneath the almond bank and soon the goats appeared around the trees, bouncing their heads around their hooves to snatch at a root amongst the rocks. The herder was amongst them, cajoling them past the terrace and up the track towards El Hacho in an old Serranían tongue. It issued from the well of his throat, cracked and split, like horse hooves treading the gravel of a dry and ancient river bed. The goats danced around him as he made his slow and arthritic steps, each one a measured act of compromise between his will and his age. He turned his brown face to the house as he passed them and dipped it low.

Some wine? said Curro as he laid a hand upon the puron, but the herder shook his head for no and didn't stop and churned his voice at his herd.

Marie took another spray of wine and opened his tobacco and shoveled some of the brittle leaf into a paper and twisted it round. He slumped against the house and smoked.

Is he still bringing you the cheese? he said and blew a heavy ring across the terrace.

When he can.

Perhaps you should ask him for a little money.

Curro stretched his legs out before him. Perhaps, he said. But we can't eat his money.

They don't sell cheese in the village now?

Last time I looked, but where's the sense in it. Why take his money to buy cheese when he'd rather give us cheese. We've enough work already.

Marie blew another ring that sat in the heavy air until it caught a fragile draft and wheeled away and broke. Probably better to make a formal arrangement though, he said.

Curro smiled. For him or us?

For us of course. He grazes them up on Hacho at least once a week. He ought to pay.

He does.

With money though, every week.

He'd only graze them somewhere else and what else would we do with the roots they pick from the rocks up there. Eat them ourselves? I'd rather have his cheese.

You should at least ask him for a kid at holy week. Roast it up.

Perhaps you should.

I will.

Curro took another stream of wine and capped it shut. Sometimes I struggle to pin you down José-Marie, he said.

How's that?

The way you look at others.

How do I look at others?

Like there's nothing in them but a way to make some money. We're all spokes on the same wheel Marie. We turn together.

Marie's face pinched. I don't think that's fair, he said sullenly.

No?

Not at all. Perhaps it's not the same for you. It's easier to fill two mouths than four.

This farm has always fed our family. It fed our grandfather's table when there were more open mouths than a nest of roqueros. Papa told us that.

Marie weighed this thoughtfully. That was a different time,

he said. People wanted for less. I need to put something down for my boys, for their boys when they come. They look to me for better things than what we had.

Like cars and televisions.

Why not? His voice was raised and the blood ran to his cheeks.

Are you still taking the car up to Ronda on the weekends for the taxi?

I am.

Does it pay well?

If the tourists are up from Málaga or Sevilla. I made a hatful last Goyesca.

Curro scratched at the grass. What did you do with it? he asked.

With what?

The hatful.

I made a few repairs and put the rest away for oil and diesel.

Curro chuckled. But if the only thing to be made on owning the car is in the keeping of the car, then what's the point in the owning of it. You don't need it for anything else. Your children go to school in the village, your wife tends the home and you could walk up here every day from Benoaján.

Francisco please, Marie pleaded. You never wanted anything more than this? He swept his hand across the terrace. Olives and almonds and peppers at harvest? Jesus knows we find enough to eat, but there has to be more to it than that. You talk about the car and say there's nothing in working to keep it if you only keep it to work it, but aren't we just the same? If all we do is work to eat, and that's as much as our work can bring, then let's go get the shotgun and save ourselves the bother.

Curro folded his hands around his knee and admired his brother's passion. With a different calling he would have gone far in this world and he pitied him the strictures of his birth.

You have convinced me, he said and reached across to pat his brother's stomach. It's no bad thing to think beyond what you see every day but I'll remind you of the thing Papa used to say.

Which was?

The man is richest whose pleasures are the cheapest. Let's try to find the balance.

Marie curled his lip as the shutters snapped hard above their heads and both men felt the siesta press upon them.

# *Four*

When he woke from the siesta his wife was gone so he laid his hand upon her pillow and caressed it slowly. Then he turned and stared at the grey outlines of the beams across the ceiling and focused his tired eyes in the dark. He lay there for a long time. When he heard the goats jangle back past the house he reproached himself for his idleness and sat up. He swung his legs off the bed and pulled his socks up from the heels and made towards the shutter and left his palm on it a while to feel the heat of the wood and pushed it back.

The valley shimmered in opaque yellow and the cordierra to the sea was its own shadow high above the white scraps of houses that stretched away from the Montejaque village, reflecting the falling sun like burnished tin. Each one piped a line of smoke into the haze and told of coffee pots and stretching limbs and sleepy children slowly coming to.

He went to the bathroom and wet his neck and then a finger and pushed it round his teeth and drank a little and descended the creaking stairs into the kitchen. His wife was working dough in a bowl with a violence that sat well upon her and he told her of it as he always did despite her disapproving glare. She fixed him coffee as he sat and brought him oil and bread and asked him if he ached.

More than usual?

From bending over the nets.

A little. My knee's not altogether right still.

Is Marie coming back up?

I told him not to.

He watched her pound the dough upon the table and then stretch it around her elbow and tamp it all back down. Her hips quivering as she worked it. A spray of flour upon her neck beneath her delicate ear. Some woman, he thought.

Come sit with me, he said.

I will.

He dropped some oil onto his plate and moved a crust through it and sucked at the rim of his cup and watched her through the steam as she slapped the dough into a deep and blackened tray. She brushed it with some oil and lifted it into the range. Then she poured her own coffee and sat across from him and cradled the cup two-handed like she did her nephews' faces for a kiss.

You've much left for the day? she asked.

I'll tidy up and have a look around.

I wonder if your friend will be waiting.

His face began to open into a smile and then stopped. I expect so, he said.

I think beneath it all you want to let him stay.

The bull? he said. And put him where?

Just let him wander.

I don't envy him his life. Jesus disgraces us all, but I'm not adopting the animals he's too drunk to feed. It'd be better for him if he just gave up and laid his head down. Bull and master both.

What is it Francisco?

What is what?

The sadness on you.

He lifted his chin and tightened his jaw. It's not sadness, he said. I've no right to be sad. Not as much as some.

You worry about the rain?

I do, but it'll come. It always does.

They sat and drank and he played at the oil on his plate with a finger.

How are we for money? he asked.

We're okay, she said and laid down the cup. It'll last to the harvest without us wanting.

And if the fruit fails?

Then we'll use what's put away.

That won't last the year.

It won't have to.

How's that?

We'll manage.

Okay then.

You can't bring the fruit in now?

There's no juice in them, he scowled. They'll fill the nets but not the jars when pressed. Another few weeks at least.

Even if the rain doesn't come?

They'll get no better without it, but it's not this year we need it for. There's nothing but dust holding the trees in. If it stays dry overwinter after a year like this they'll struggle to stay standing come spring.

You exaggerate.

Some. It's been known though.

Is it worse for us?

He nodded. Always has been. There's less to hold them down on Hacho than further down the valley and the wind picks at the slopes up here.

Would you swap it?

I couldn't if I wanted to.

She reached across the table and laid her hands on his and stroked the ridges of his knuckles, her fingers cresting the peaks and massaging the softer flesh between them.

We'll be okay, she said.

I don't doubt it.

What are you going to do?

If the stove is on for bread, I'll throw a little almond in.

She smiled warmly.

Good, she said. I'm enjoying the company. There's a pan full on the terrace and they'll be soaked through now.

He patted her hand and stood from the table and walked in his stockinged feet to the door and pushed it open. A warm breeze lifted his fringe and there was a calmness to the world. He stepped to the terrace and came around it and tilted his head to Hacho's peak where griffon vultures wheeled upon a thermal, scanning the slopes for prey. A pale sickle moon hung against the lavender sky. He found the pan amongst the claywork pots with the almonds sitting proudly within, like pebbles in a shallow brook. He plucked one out and shook the water loose and tested it with his teeth and knew that they were right.

He kicked his feet into his boots at the door and passed into the pantry where he found the tray and strainer and took them both back out. He arranged the pan on the lip of the terrace and sat astride it and scooped at the almonds with the strainer and took them up and placed a hand across them while he shook them dry. Then he ladled them onto a light cotton cloth upon the tray and when the tray was full he took the cloth around the almonds and bundled it into a sack. He wrung the neck and swung the sack around and when the moisture pierced the cloth he clattered them out across the tray. He gently spread them out with his fingers like a pianist warming on a scale and pressed the cloth back on them and left it there awhile.

Over the almond bank he could see the road curling away from the cortijo and join the one that came from the Montejaque village before looping through the valley and tracing the river up to the plateau and then to Ronda. A pair of caballeros, in full dress trotted proudly past the junction, the riders handsome and erect with the one hand holding the reins aloft and the other cupped upon the knee. A train of cars waited for them to pass and then edged around them deferentially and the drivers waved and Curro nodded his approval because the traditions of the land still commanded such respect.

He pressed the cloth again and satisfied the stones were dry he took the tray into the kitchen. His wife was paring aubergines but stopped when he entered and handed him a pot of rock salt. The kitchen was her domain but the ritual of the almonds was only ever his. There had never been a time in which he could remember a woman of the house prepare the almonds. His father had been adamant that they mastered the stove in all respects but this one.

The first time Curro had walked his future wife up from her home in Benoaján to meet the family his father had sat them down when the plates were cleared and pulled a tray of browning stones from the range and showed his pride at their brittle succulence. Women always burn them, he'd laughed, or drown them in salt and he cracked his hand across the rump of his wife to make his point. His wife had threatened him with the spoon to spur the game and insisted that almonds were a harmless enough thing to trust a man with. She never deigned to make them herself though and when Curro's wife made the same kitchen her own, she understood and accepted the tradition.

Curro tipped a little of the rock salt into a marble mortar and ground it rhythmically with a wooden handled pestle of the same stone. Then he pinched at the dusted salt and dressed the almonds lightly, stopping once to rotate them on the tray. He took a single almond from the bed and pressed his tongue upon it and turned it around and masticated it thoroughly.

They're good, he said and rubbed his palms together to frisk them free of salt and wiped them clean upon his trouser hips and then he reached for a cloth and wrapped it around the black iron of the range door.

Curro! she hissed. It was enough to make him pause and he looked at her blankly.

The bread.

Of course, he said. You'll put the almonds in when it's risen?

I could, but where are you going?

Nowhere.

Then wait and put it in yourself.

# *Five*

Jose-Marie eased the car into a vacant space under the shade of the pinsapo firs which cool the Plaza de Ayuntamiento and passed through the cobbled warren of the cuidad until he came to the Tajo mirador. There he sat on a warm stone bench and breathed the jasmine that freckled the heavy smell of the leather from the artisan galleries and watched the tourists point and marvel at the view beyond the Ronda gorge. A guitarist laced the air with a melancholy riff which rose and fell away into the gulf beyond the ornate railings of the mirador.

The tourists clasped their hands together and swayed their heads as they passed in gratified silence. Most were elderly and elegantly clad in crisp linen suits and finely knitted shawls with polished shoes that clicked percussively upon the cobbles. Marie watched them come and pass and drop their coins into the musician's hat and let his envies harden.

He left the bench and crossed the mirador and continued onto the Puente Nuevo where he paused to crane his head over the bridge to see how low the water was. Then he walked amongst the restaurant terraces that clustered around the Plaza de Toros, now thronged with spirited diners picking gambas clean and clinking fragile crystal flutes together. He passed the bronzework of Pedro Romero and tipped his hat to his memory and met the swarm of bodies spread across the Bola, the artery of commerce linking the cuidad to the mercadillo and the old world to the new.

Children ran amongst the legs of people making their slow paseo from bar to bar, like his own did amongst the rows of peas on the family cortijo and all were dressed like his own could never hope to be. Shop doors were flung open wide to attract cooler air and pesetas to the heaving rows of electronic goods and fine cigars and souvenir foods. He slipped past them all and made a turn into the Calle Monterejas. He continued to the intersection where a line of taxis idled with their drivers leaning upon them and he nodded an acknowledgement as he pushed at the door of the bar.

Inside the air was fat with smoke that pooled around the ceiling in opulent reefs and stung his eyes and throat. The television sprayed the darkened walls with brightly coloured fans as the Sevilla corrida was replayed to little interest from those who came to drink and pick apart the day. He pressed some palms and took some heavy slaps across his shoulders as he slimmed himself towards the bar.

Tinto grande, he said and took it quickly in his hand and drank.

Antonio! he said and pushed his glass across the bar which bore the heavily tattooed stains of many nights past. The wine came and Antonio asked him if he'd eat.

Whatever's fresh and cheap, said Marie. But then the memory of gambas and steaks, scarlet rare in their blood from the Plaza de Toros and the ornate bowls of pate that came as garnish to the meals for mouths with better teeth than his made him wonder why for once he shouldn't have it so.

Wait, he said and waved him back. Bring me two sides of pata negra and when my company arrives, I'll take a tray of langoustines and a half of cava with two glasses.

Langoustines and cava? Antonio said and frowned and smiled simultaneously. Where do you think you are? I've got merluza on the skewer and a viura from Logroño.

Marie shrugged and nodded. Bring them to the table when he arrives, he said.

You disappoint me Marie, said Antonio.

Why?

I thought it was a she.

Then I disappoint us both.

Antonio grinned and disappeared behind the beaded curtain to the kitchen. Marie eased along the bar and took a table in the alcove beneath the television set. He rolled a cigarette and dipped his lips into the wine and smoked. His pata negra came and he chewed it slowly and then he smoked some more. He was deep in conversation with another olive man from La Chavera when he caught a whistle from Antonio who was waving a fat man in a suit and neck-tie to his table.

Marie stood and grasped the man's hand and pumped it hard. Señor Hernandez, he said and looked deeply into his eyes. Have you eaten?

Hernandez confirmed he had but patted his round and ample shirt front and laughed that a little room could still be found for more. Marie snapped his fingers at the bar and bade him to a stool and asked him of the road from Málaga.

Steep and long, Hernandez said and placed a leather satchel down upon the table as he balanced his bulk upon the stool. He pinched the clasp of the satchel and spread the documents between them.

# *Six*

They woke together and lay and listened to the birds squabbling in the almond grove in the first light of dawn and held each other's hands and didn't need to talk. She briefly slipped asleep again and came back round but still her hand was encased in his. She stroked the length of his thumb with her own and listened to his sonorous breath fill the little room until she thought he'd drifted off and then attempted to release her grip but he flinched and held it tighter still.

A moment more, he whispered.

I have to pee.

You'll not burst for a moment more.

She wriggled her hand free but didn't leave and turned and laid her head upon his chest and grazed his cheek with wisps of hair raked free from her bun during the night. He pulled her closer under his arm and clasped her thigh and pawed at it through the sheer membrane of her nightdress and they lay in their docility until his arm began to ache and her swollen bladder forced her out from underneath the sheet.

She fixed him coffee which he took with his boots and hat onto the terrace where he sat on the lip and watched the sun embroider the ridge of the eastern valley wall with a liquid amber string. Soon it crested it completely but the sweat was upon him long before the hot dry sheet of light descended. He fiddled at his laces and took his coffee slowly and thought of the day and the work that would fill it. Marie wasn't due for most of an hour so he thought to check his traps until his brother came.

He returned the cup to the kitchen and lifted his trapping satchel from the hook behind the pantry door and soaked a crust of moist warm bread with oil and split a ripe tomato upon it with a grind of pepper and a pinch from the salt bowl. He ate as he walked the track from the cortijo down through the almond grove to the Montejaque road. There he walked to the north, away from the village where the road followed the perimeter of his land until it curved around the limestone columns guarding the head of the reservoir. When he rounded them he saw the crater of the reservoir and its desolate, lunar emptiness, the tiny, huddled flaps of muddy water at its centre far beneath the band of brown high-water marks that ringed the taller slopes.

He trudged on down the road, until the tall dead grasses swaying in the hot morning breeze gave way to clumps of tangled brush and oak, the trees stripped of their bark for wine cork and left with blood red throats the colour of the wine itself. He left the road and followed a track into the forest and cast his mind to where he'd set the traps some days before. He usually snapped a branch above the trap to tell of where it lay and soon he came upon one.

The noose was tight around a coiled pyre of bones and fur and blood encrusted entrails calcified by the sun. The head was intact and the shriveled eyes were beads of fear. He carefully brushed the debris of twigs and grass around the site to identify the tracks of the fox or ibex whose meal he had supplied but the wind had washed it clean. He never cursed such a thing, given as he was to recognising the superiority of the hunters against whom he pitted his own wiles and he admitted to himself that their need outweighed his own.

Within the hour he'd forged a loop through the forest and kicked the dust upon three more stripped carcasses but not before he'd found two fresh ones unmolested by the competition. He bagged them and reset the traps and took the path behind the reservoir which bought him over the northern slopes of Hacho and back upon the cortijo.

His wife was sucking an orange clean beneath the kitchen window when he passed her on the terrace. She noted the bulge of the trapping sack and circled her hand to inspect the quarry. He dug them out and passed them over and she felt around the meat of the thigh and needled her fingers into their bellies and stroked the length of the ears and smiled and pursed her lips with approval and told him where to put them.

Most of them were stripped in their traps, he said and tapped the toe of his boots against the wall to free the dust.

There's enough to go round.

I wasn't complaining.

I know it.

He took them through the kitchen into the pantry and wrapped them in newspaper and bound them tight with string before hooking them through their ankles to the wall. When he returned upon the terrace he flinched at the hot slap of the sun whose hand seemed to be becoming heavier with the passing of autumn and he wondered how it could be so.

Never in my born days can I remember it so intense so late, he said despairingly. It's like God himself has abandoned this valley to the devil and refuses to turn the wheel to winter.

It hasn't evaporated your sense of drama though, she chuckled. We should be thankful of that.

You don't have to work in it, he growled, but he knew she'd wear it better than he if she did. They often said she was the Moor to his Reconquista in their Andalusian confection for her tolerance of the heat.

She stood and pinched his arm then rubbed the imaginary wound and leaned upon him for a kiss.

We've seen it so before, she said. We're just getting older. Remember the year we married and we wanted to ride to Algeciras to see the sea. We only made it to Gaucin before the horses buckled under the sun. We never thought we'd make it back, you remember that I know. I was giddy with the heat and only just a girl.

But that was the top of the summer, stupid as we were, he said. Look at this. He wafted his hand accusingly across the valley. It's November soon and it's hotter than hell imagined.

You want to saddle up and try again? she teased. Paco would lend us the horses for it.

I doubt I'd make it to Paco's, much less Algeciras.

I'm not talking about Algeciras. I mean to head for the cave just off the Gaucin road where we sheltered from the sun. Where the stream came through the rocks enough to soak our feet and we lay for hours under the pines waiting for night until it was cool enough to go back up.

We never did, he said.

I remember how long it took you to make a fire in that cave.

I remember the way you looked wrapped in that blanket. He paused. Just a blanket and not a stitch beneath. The fire in your eyes.

I never loved you more.

He closed his eyes enough to let the sun filter though the heavy lashes and smiled the way a man who feels he never wasted a moment in his life might do, because he has a memory of such a thing.

I've never seen it still, he said.

What?

The sea.

I know. We'll take the train to Conil when the fruit is in.

We say it every year.

I know it, she said. This year we'll do it too. We have less time left to us than those two silly kids in the cave.

I'll hold you to it.

I want you to.

He stood square to her and held her by the shoulders and pulled her close.

Too hot for all that, she said and patted his chest affectionately. Are you ready to make siesta or are you poking around some more?

I've not been sleeping well, he mused. I'll not bother today.

Your own choice. For me, it's too hot not to. She stepped up to the house and turned. What will you do? You're not working in this.

There's a little project I need to think about. I'll take the shade up in the grove and see about working it out.

Never without your intrigues Curro, she said as she passed on through the door.

He fastened his hat to his brow and turned the collar of his shirt and walked away from the terrace towards El Hacho and the olives that sweltered beneath its imperious heights. He kicked through the dust to the foot of the mountain where the trees submitted to the gradient and he continued to a ledge that his father had excavated from the loose rock. Here, a thin granite sheaf, whipped by the sun and wind had split and fallen and lodged itself perpendicular to the slopes to form a roof and cool a space which gave a view to the whole valley.

He hopped awkwardly over the rocks underneath the ledge and saw the bull a hundred metres further down but still inside his own land, a long blank lozenge immobile and nestled in a low screen of brush.

Why doesn't he escape the heat, he thought, and knew he was the bull himself. The thought stayed with him long after he had settled into the ledge and refused to cede to any other until he leaned forward and massaged his eyes.

The project, he said aloud and scanned the grove. An ochre track twisted though it, knotted into kinks like the bubbled veins behind his own knees and slipped out of sight where the land fell away towards the reservoir. For years he had minded to level out the ruts and pave it flat to ease the task of harvest but had always found the excuses not to. There was always too much work to do before harvest and not enough motivation thereafter, so the ruts grew deeper and the harvest harder still.

For stone he would dismantle the decrepit walls that at one time had bordered the track and divided his family plot from a neighbour's before his great grandfather had acquired the land and united the groves into one. The structure of the walls had eroded over time but the stone lay fast in its constituent parts ready to be used again. Curro had no need for the wall.

He had no illusions about the scale of the task nor the sweat he would lose over it, but like other men powerless to affect the thing that they desired the most, he deputised another task to stop his hands from idling while he waited.

Maybe God would reward his efforts with some rain. He also thought of Marie and his recent lack of application and hoped they would unite over some honest work and sew together some of the space that had opened between them.

He stretched his legs and yawned and peeped out from the cave to see the bull but it had vanished. He lowered his back to step under the roof and trod upon the stones before it and as he danced down the slope he made them clink and sing like the pipits in the almond trees at dawn.

# *Seven*

He rose in the black of night and trod with care so as not to wake her. He washed around his neck in the kitchen sink and filled a leather gourd with water and ripped a loaf and placed it with some fruit into his trapping satchel. He thought of sitting for coffee before he left and made to clear the pot but changed his mind for fear his motivation would desert him if he did. He stepped out onto the blue cool of the terrace with his boots and sat on the lip and laced them up and craned his neck at a ripe moon that softly washed the contours of the valley and enjoyed the vault of silence which found a space between the end of the insects and start of the birds. His breath the only sound.

He walked carefully to the stable block and released the latch and groped around the shelving for some matches and struck one and waved it over his head to find his gloves. He found them on a hook behind the door and dropped the match and pulled them on. They were cured and stiff and the leather pinched the fleshy web beneath his thumb as he balled his fists and fanned his fingers out to make them supple.

They'll work back in, he said and fastened the latch behind him as he left.

He found the track and set his satchel down beside him where the stone lay. Above him El Hacho shone in the moonlight. He sat on his calves and released his gloves and ran his hands across the undulations of the earth. Then he cupped a palm of dust and let it fall between his fingers and then walked to where a clump of rocks lay beneath the remains of the wall and lifted one, no bigger than a melon, to test the weight.

He had already worked out the method. He would pile the rocks into little mounds according to their size at intervals along the track. Large rocks to fill the deeper ruts and establish a base and the smaller ones to cement the gaps. Only when all the stones were piled would he then begin to set them. Encouraged by the simplicity of this initial task he found his gloves and pulled them tight and bent his back and worked.

Within an hour he had piled three mounds of equal size and the sweat washed his temples and cooled in the pre-dawn breeze. He had made twenty metres on his satchel and he walked back to it and pulled the water out and drank. When he stood and turned to see his work he caught the milky pink-tinged frost of dawn penciled across the ridges of the slopes above the reservoir and Hacho's eastern flank and knew the sun was coming.

Just once, he said bitterly. Just one day without you on my back, you bitch. But as he said the words and felt the acrid seed swell within him he straightened himself and shook his head in reprove.

When will you learn Francisco? he muttered. You can no more will the rain to come than you can the arthritis from your knees. Concentrate your energies on the things they can achieve and leave the rest to God. Aware he was speaking aloud alone, he twisted his head nervously to ensure he was so and spat into the gloves and started on another mound.

The birds were fidgeting in the olives and he was glad of the company when they began to chatter around him. The ivory light of the moon was soon displaced by the fresh clarity of the sun's own light as it speared between the mountains of the eastern cordillera and forced him back to the satchel to drink.

He worked and the great angry ball rose above him ruthlessly as he heaved the rock and he pulled down the buttons of his shirt front inversely to its height and weight and he vowed through spittled lips not to let it master him. The gloves became malleably warm and stained with the ink of his sweat and filmed with a fine ochre dust. The pinch at the base of his spine spread up it slowly and clawed at his shoulders until he knew he had to stop and rest. He collapsed against the gnarled base of an olive truck and filled his chest with hot air. The gourd was empty and his stomach groaned but he counted thirty mounds in all and his satchel was a brown speck back down the track.

Beyond the satchel he saw his wife appear before the house and stand on her toes to see across the almond bank, her image warped by the rising heat from the land. Then she began to twist and shape with the excited vigour of a sapling thrashing in the wind and the merry pitch of children's voices echoed up the track. When her nephews arrived on the terrace he watched her lift them from the floor by their necks to drown them in her kisses and set them back down and rub their arms and hair and hold her knees to bend close to them in exaggerated attention and listen to their news. Then he saw Marie vault up next to her and peck her cheek and she spread her hands and lifted her shoulders and pointed aimfully up to where Curro sat watching.

Marie waved the children into the house where something sweet awaited them and strode past the stable block and up the track with the cool, purposeful languor of a Grazalema lynx making its rounds at dusk. When he found his brother crumpled against an olive he looked at him warily and turned to regard the strange monuments of stone along the path and faced him again with a crooked smile.

What are you doing? he asked.

Resting.

And these? He turned upon the rocks again.

They're resting too.

Marie squinted up at Hacho and hooked his thumbs into his belt loops and said, are we working today?

I've been working since before the dawn.

On this? Another glance back down the track. What's it for?

A little project I've been putting off for too long. Curro eased himself afoot and leaned against the olive trunk for support. His muscles were tight and heavy and his tongue fat in his mouth. Have you any water in that satchel?

Some wine.

Give it to me.

Marie unclasped the satchel slowly and handed him a blackened puron. Curro took a measure and swilled it round his teeth and spat it into the dust. Then he drank.

You want to hear it? he said, wiping his mouth with his hand.

What?

The project.

Of course.

You can't work it out by looking?

Do I have to?

No.

Then tell me.

Curro straightened his back and pushed himself from the olive trunk. You know how much we complain about this track when we're in the thick of it at harvest and it takes the both of us to push the cart through these ruts.

Marie grunted.

We always say we'll mend it but we never do. The longer we leave it the worse it gets and the more we complain. So let us mend it.

Marie's eyes widened until the blood showed around the rims and he stared at his brother with his mouth agape in bewilderment.

In this heat, he cried. Are you crazy?

What else can we do while we wait for the rain to swell this fruit? The nets are repaired, the tools are oiled, the sun has burnt up the vegetable garden and I grow old too fast when I sit around idling. We can start early and make a long siesta and then come back to it later on. Come on, let's bend our backs and make use of the time, rather than sitting around and cursing the weather.

Marie slithered around uncomfortably and fetched his cap from his head and beat it against his leg and scratched at his thinning hair and twisted his face into sore little scowls.

You think it's a bad idea? Curro asked.

It's a good idea to get the track paved, but not to kill ourselves in the paving of it.

What's the fuss? We'll take our time and keep out of the sun and it'll come together nicely. Maybe we only do a section of it this year before the harvest comes and finish it later when the fruit has been pressed. And how else do we do it, if not by our own hand?

Marie dropped his head thoughtfully. If we buy a tractor, the state of the track doesn't matter.

Oh, a tractor, yes, that's a good idea. And after that we'll buy an aeroplane and fly to somewhere nice. And maybe I'll send Carmen up to Ronda and she can buy every dress on the Bola and a silk suit for me. He shook his head at his younger brother. You know what Papa used to tell us when things got a little tight?

Marie gave him a tough stare, stung by his sarcasm and asked him what.

Pay when you have the money, work when you have the time.

Marie sagged and shuffled his feet and drew his arms to his hips and made to speak and lost himself in the thought.

What good did it do him? he said.

Curro hardened his jaw and narrowed his eyes and looked beyond Marie to where their parent's grave sat at the entrance to the grove.

The work or the wisdom? he said.

Them both.

You think he died a pauper?

Marie raised his hands to the sky and weighed an invisible weight and tilted his head and sighed.

Who knows Curro, and who cares? he said. I know what you're going to tell me, because I've been hearing it for years. You're going to say there's more to riches than money and more nobility in the sweat of life than in the watching of it pass you by without sweating, but the more I hear it the less it means to me.

Ok, you have your point, Curro smiled. I've become predictable. He patted his brother's stomach with the back of his hand as he passed him. The rocks of the nearest mound had listed untidily and fallen around in the dust. He lifted his head to Marie as he bent to tidy them.

Why are the children not at school? he said. You had me thinking it's a Saturday.

The teacher has a fever.

There's not another?

They tell us no.

Carmen will be pleased.

They'll learn more with her anyway.

It's the truth, Curro said reflectively. He stood and took a handkerchief and folded it neatly and swabbed the back of his neck and squinted at the sun beneath the crook of his arm and judged the hour from its angle over the valley and replaced the cloth in his pocket.

So, we do a few hours on this? he asked.

Curro, I'm not sure.

Of what? You have better plans?

Marie stared at the rusting grass that trembled gently at the foot of the olive and did not answer. Then he fidgeted with his hands and shifted his weight between his feet and rolled his eyes from rock to tree and back to the grass and did not meet Curro's gaze for such a time that Curro was moved to laugh. He was no stranger to his brother's lethargy, but his excuses were habitually immediate and plain.

Are you mute? You look sick.

Marie's cheeks had blanched but his eyes were blackened by trouble and he swallowed hard and scratched his throat, but still he didn't answer.

Jose-Marie! Out with it! Curro demanded and approached him slowly.

Marie shuffled back along the track and scooped his satchel from the floor and showed his palm to stay his brother and shook his head and cleared his throat.

Not today, he said, I can't work today. I can't. Almudena will be up to collect the children for siesta and I'll come back up tomorrow. I'm sorry.

He scuttled down the track towards the house, tripping awkwardly in the cleft surface. Bewildered, Curro returned to his stones and his labour and the puron of wine warmed slowly in the brown grass.

# *Eight*

For a further five days Curro worked the track alone, appearing in the grove an hour before the light and returning after the long siesta when the venom had been drawn from the sun. He had arranged the stones by nightfall on the third day and set to paving it the following morning but had made slow progress since then.

Jose-Marie's continued absence had began as just a puzzle and then became the object of the shallow breathed curses Curro spat whilst he worked, but soon he came to realise that something extraordinary must have come to pass to keep his brother away. As the cramp in his knotted muscles worsened and the pain across his back increased, the unpaved track of red dust winding through the olives did not appreciably shorten and he knew he wouldn't be able to finish it alone.

God loves the willing, he mumbled as he slumped against

the trunk of an olive, but he knew that will alone was not enough and he sat and stared at the implacable face of El Hacho above him. As he shifted his weight to ease the pinch on his spine he felt the tree move with him and so he pulled himself to his knees and rested his palm against the warm bark and pushed it firmly. It creaked and tilted back and the earth around the base, nothing but sand and flinty pebbles, stirred as the roots writhed beneath. A cold horror clutched at his stomach and he brought his fingers to his lips and raked at the stubble on his chin with their calloused tips. He pushed the tree again and dared to watch it tip gently forward and rock back towards him.

These trees won't see Christmas, he said with rattling breath and for the first time since the onset of the drought he found himself truly scared of what it might do to his land and to his living. He stood and nipped a fruit from the tree and pressed it gently and frowned and ground his nail into its feeble flesh and cast it down amongst the dust despondently. He looked around the grove and up across the lower slopes of Hacho's flank and down across the valley to the south and saw the whole of the land heave a singular, terrible, beseeching lament for rain.

His wife was waving to him from the terrace and he waved back to her through leaden arms. She beckoned him towards the house with febrile, agitated movements so he gathered his satchel and shook the bread crumbs from the wax paper and wrapped it around the empty gourd and put them both into the bag. The work had shaped his gloves into a claw and he gathered them and beat them free of dust against his legs as he walked.

She met him on the terrace and fussed over his aches and took his satchel and rough palms in hers and worked her thumbs into the knots and kissed the split and broken nails and said that they must eat a rabbit she had stuffed with sage and garlic and sit and talk awhile. He let her lead him to the kitchen where they sat and ate and stayed till late.

# *Nine*

The next morning he slept till late and didn't work but busied himself amongst the vegetable patch and took some flowers to his parent's grave. In the afternoon he soaked some almonds and sat on the lip of the terrace and shared a coffee with his wife and called a greeting to the cork men hauling their empty carts up past the cortijo along the reservoir road. He sat and stared and time passed by until he saw the same men return with loads of precious bark. Then he made a long siesta.

He rose around seven and salted his almonds and ate a stew of potatoes and onion before he shaved and sat in a bath for long after the water had cooled. Then he took a freshly laundered shirt from his wife, a little frayed at the cuffs but immaculately clean and smartly pressed and fetched his best jacket from the wardrobe and matched some trousers to it and shined the shoes he kept for Easter Mass. He accepted the compliments on his appearance from his wife and kissed her strongly about the neck and tipped some coins from a wooden tankard above the stove into his jacket pocket and closed the kitchen door behind him.

He stepped through the almond grove carefully so as not to raise the dust and turned upon the Barriada de Santiago towards the Montejaque village. The heat radiated from the road as powerfully as it did from the sun at noon despite it having dipped beyond the valley wall and the sweat stood on his brow.

Between the cortijo and the first houses of the village, with Hacho watching him over his right shoulder, he passed a motley stand of self-set olives and wild bush vines, the fruit stripped by resourceful children long before they'd showed their best. Patch after patch of monstrous agave lined his route, their viscous spear-tipped leaves rising and falling like Medusa's snakes. Sprouting from cracks in the uneven pavement and lodged impossibly into pockets of dust in the gutter were the fragile orange flowers of the Grazalema poppy, thirsting for the rain that had given them life and then cruelly deserted them.

At the junction of the Calle Nueva he thought to take a mouth of water from the trough but the pipes had ceased to flow and the bowl was empty. Never in my born days, he thought, have I seen this bowl without water and he continued along the Avenida Andalucía with a troubled mind.

As he entered the Plaza de la Constitucion he was recognised immediately by the oracles of village life who always sat there at that hour. They waved him to them and asked him why he came so seldom to share a view on things. He laughed awhile and pressed some palms and shook his head with them about the rain and asked them all if he could wet their lips with something but they preferred to sit and catch a breeze and watch the children chirp and run amongst the cars and carts and orange trees.

Another time then, he said and waved to their wives who sat on wicker chairs before the doorways of their homes and gossiped above their knitting. He walked on towards the shuttered windows of the Bodega del Pueblo. Inside a grumbling fan above the door circulated stale, warm air and the bar was empty save for the owner and a teenage couple sharing an intimate tapas. As Curro approached the bar the owner folded his arms and his flat white teeth broke his copper cheeks.

Currito, he said. I thought you were just a rumour.

It's been a while, Curro admitted. I've been waiting on new ownership.

Me too. What shall we have?

I'll take some wine.

Cask or a bottle?

Whatever's best.

The owner laughed and stretched to the rack above the till for an unlabeled bottle gilded with gold mesh. And put that money back in your pocket before I get upset, he said.

He corked the bottle and filled two tumblers, threw his drink down quickly and laid his hands across the wooden bar.

Curro drank carefully and accepted the bottle again. You're the last of your type Diego, he said.

Yet still I'm poor. You want to play a little chess? You can see how busy I am.

I'd like to but it's my brother that I've come for.

Then you've time for a game. If horses still shit where they stand he'll be here before long.

You think it?

Diego nodded. I set my watch by him. When he comes, it's ten or thereabouts.

That's good. I'll wait.

Diego stooped below the counter to reach a box of polished eucalyptus that rattled as he moved it. Then he lifted the lid and tipped out the pieces, small and crudely hewn from soapstone and began to arrange them on the board which folded from the box.

A pretty set, said Curro, squeezing a piece gently between thumb and forefinger the way he would test an olive's ripeness.

You know Andrés, the Catalan? Diego asked.

From Atajate?

He had a shop there but he couldn't make it work. Now he lives on the Calle Consejeo.

I know him by name only.

He couldn't pay his bill so he offered me the set.

What does he do now?

Drinks and spits about the General most days.

It's an easy choice.

Easier for some. You want to start?

Your pleasure, said Curro and spun the board so that the line of ebony pieces arrayed at his elbows.

Diego poured more wine and lit the stump of a cigar and chewed through the smoke as he parried his opponent's predictable opening moves. Curro was never much of a player although he always found the game a useful distraction from the troubled thoughts that lay upon his mind and he was becoming pleasantly lost within it as the bar slowly populated around him. Soon a hand clasped his shoulder.

Guillermo, said Curro and showed the man a warm smile as he bellied up to their game.

Curro. How is it?

Better for him, said Curro, flicking a finger at Diego who was turning his attention between the board and the needs of his clients. He has both my horses already.

A bandit this one, Guillermo laughed as he reached over the wide oak slab and pulled a tumbler from underneath the lip and held it to the light to check the smears. Satisfied, he set it down and clasped the bottle and poured it to the rim. He took it in a strong hand and showed the dirt in his nails and the bands of grease across his cuffs. He raised it with a little ceremony and made to toast, but stopped and turned and sighed.

Curro, he said. I can't think of a thing to drink to.

No?

No.

Your family at least.

They'll ruin me before this weather. A boy who should be helping but sits around the house afraid to bend his back and a daughter whose only ambition is to turn into her mother. God help them, and me. I'd rather drink to this heat.

Let's just drink to drink then.

It's all there is, Guillermo agreed and yanked a mouthful back. He swabbed his mouth and studied the board. Your move?

Curro nodded and allowed his friend to move a pawn to defend a play he hadn't seen.

How's your fruit? Guillermo said. You must be suffering up there.

Ah, said Curro and narrowed his eyes. I saw something today that made me shiver.

Yes?

It's not a pleasant tale.

Tell it anyway.

Curro stiffened on his stool and cleared his throat to speak.

My father used to talk of the times when he would sit around the stove with his sisters on a winter's night and suck the salt off an almond and listen to his own father's memories from the farm. He told a tale of way back sometime, must've been before the war for it to be my grandfathers time at Hacho, when the summer wouldn't end and just kept pushing on and on till way past Christmas and the reservoir was down to mud and they were rioting up near Madrid because of the way the harvest pushed the price of bread up.

I remember him telling it, as clearly as I see this glass I'm holding. His father had come down one morning from his bed and there was a mist lying up the valley and he remembered it because he thought there might be a little rain behind it so he took his hat and stick and went a walk up on Hacho to get a better view of the cordillera and when he got there he sat on this little bench that's sheltered by a fallen slab. It's the same place I go from time to time if I want to think something straight. By the time my grandfather had finished the apple he'd taken up there with him the mist had lifted and beneath it all the trees lay flat on their sides like some fallen army on the battlefield. Every one on its side, roots bare to the world.

My father told us that story more than once and there was a twinkle to the way he told it that made me think he'd just made it up to warn Marie and I not to waste the water the way you do when you are kids and you get hold of the hose. I never thought it a possibility until today when I leant back on a tree and felt it rock back and forth and watched the roots move around in the soil. Another week of this and they'll be on their arse and so will I.

The soil has always been thinner up there Curro, said Guillermo, slowly circling his finger around the rim of his empty glass. You should have planted vines. They flourish in nothing.

What do I know about wine?

Guillermo shrugged. My patch is dry and the fruit has a way to go but the trees are still well set. Are you sure it wasn't a dead one.

I know my grove, said Curro proudly. Last year that tree dropped three full sacks on its own.

Diego appeared from behind the curtain to the kitchen and slapped a towel across his shoulder and set another bottle next to the chess board. Then he fingered his queen across the board and smiled thinly and pulled the cork. Drink, he said. And checkmate.

Curro reviewed the pieces and frowned and reached across the bar for Diego's palm.

What did I tell you? Guillermo said. A bandit. Then he took the bottle and poured the glasses out.

Diego looked beyond them both and then at Curro and held aloft his watch and tapped the face and said, I told you so.

The watch read a five past ten.

Curro twisted on his stool and met the melancholy glare of his brother.

# Ten

Jose-Marie lingered in the doorway with a week of stubble standing on his chin and his face reddened by the drink to a violet hue that the sun alone could never make. He seemed set to stay there indefinitely until a queue formed behind him and pressed him forward as they passed.

Marie, said Guillermo, darting his hand toward him. Have a glass and take a game with us. Your brother is down one already.

He was never much of a player.

It's true, Guillermo laughed and slapped Curro's thigh playfully and turned back to Marie. Did you see the corrida at Toledo?

Marie slipped between them and lifted the bottle to feel its weight and shook it slightly and cocked his head at Diego for a tumbler and took it when it came and filled it halfway and studied the colour before he drank.

I caught the last one, he said. Castrovenjas I think it was. He made a mess of it.

He has none of his father's grace, Guillermo admitted.

He prances around like he's Manolito though, said Marie. The bull looked like he'd been through a thresher by the time he finished it.

The crowd let him know it. Did you see it Francisco?

Curro was arranging the pieces for a fresh game but without any real intent and stopped and fingered his tumbler but set it down without drinking.

No.

He hasn't a television up there, said Marie staring forward at the rack of dusty bottles above the sink.

Who has the time to watch it?

Good luck to you Curro, said Guillermo. I only have one in the house to cover the sound of her squawking. He poured another level of wine and stood and secured his hat to his ears and tipped his wrist and rolled the wine about his tongue.

To which I must return. The later I am, the louder it gets. I'll see you both again. Diego! he shouted to the curtain. Until tomorrow!

Diego issued a response through the beads from the muddy light of the kitchen and Guillermo rolled through the door into the square.

Marie slumped his frame against the bar and maintained his view of the rack. Curro patted the bottle. Let us take it to the corner and talk a little, he said. Marie nodded his head expectantly.

They passed around the bar and took a table by the window and sat and smiled a greeting to the young couple who played with each other's hands above the remnants of their food.

Curro leaned back against the chair and waited until Marie was settled.

You look like life's living all over you little brother, he said. Why are you drinking so much?

Marie's face darkened but he did not answer.

Curro continued. I'd say that taxi of yours is beginning to pay if you can soak it up in here every night but I know you've not been taking it out.

It needs new tyres.

That's what I know.

Marie shrugged and poured the wine and drank it back and pulled at his ear lobe and scanned the room through sad, tired eyes.

So what brings you down here tonight Francisco? It's not the chess.

No.

No.

Although I'd like to play more often.

I'm sure.

No, I thought I'd come and help you to tell me what it is that's making you drink instead of work.

What makes you think I have something to tell?

Curro breathed deeply and smiled and pressed his palms together and shook his head gracefully.

I *know*, Jose-Marie. You don't think your wife talks to mine about the things that cause her concern? And before you turn your anger on her, you must know I have none for you. Only some sadness that you feel ashamed to tell it to me.

I'm not ashamed.

Then let us talk.

Marie ground his teeth and took a long, slow drink.

It's the best opportunity we'll ever see Francisco, he said. The best. If I didn't tell you so far it's because I wanted it straight in my own mind first.

And now you have it straight.

Yes.

Which company is it?

Hernandez, Molina and Sons.

And what is their offer?

Marie reached inside his jacket and pulled a folded piece of paper, smudged with grey at the folds and plucked it open and passed it across the table. Curro took it and read it slowly and nodded his head knowingly as he did. Then he folded it back and set it down between the tumblers.

A handsome offer.

I think so.

And what will we do with the money?

Marie became enlivened for the first time, a flicker emerging through the bloodstained eyes.

Whatever we like, he said. Think of it Curro, a house up in Ronda, or even Malaga if we like. A car, a proper, new car, that doesn't sick its oil every time you turn the engine and plenty left to spare. Better clothes, better food. A good school for Raul and Quique.

But what will *we* do, Jose Marie? When we leave our fine house in our fine cars in the morning, in our good clothes. What will we do to fill our time and earn our bread? That number on the paper there looks good in ink, but wouldn't last us five years before we had to lift our hands again.

Marie deflated on his chair and rolled his head around and passed his hand across his brow and pulled it down over his face and raked at the stubble beneath his mouth.

I'm tired Curro, he said quietly. I'm exhausted by it all, the daily grind of life up there. I think a man reserves the right to change his life if it isn't what he wants and the chance to change it comes along.

It saddens you this much?

Marie nodded despairingly. It does.

Curro filled his chest and spoke benignly. You are my younger brother and I love you, he said, the tears behind his eyes. There is no shame in what you say. Lift up your head and look at me.

Marie raised his eyes and blinked slowly.

For a very long time I've known that this life wasn't for you. Since you were barely older than your own two boys and I bear some responsibility for trying to make you into what you are not. Perhaps it is my own vanity, my own stubborn insecurities that prevented me from encouraging you to leave the farm and shape your own life as you see fit and it would be a betrayal of my love for you if I prevented it now.

But I will not sell the land to Hernandez, Molina and Sons, nor any other company like them and I will tell you why.

I am a farmer Jose-Marie. An olive man from Montejaque. Our father was an olive man from Montejaque and so was his father's father. You might say I lack ambition but that land is an extension of my own body. I could no more leave it than tear the tongue from my mouth. When I work it I stir the memory of our people into the fragile dust and every drop of sweat, every callous on my hand and groan in my joints is theirs as well as mine. To abandon it would be to abandon myself and that I cannot do. But I have other reasons.

This is not the first time a man from Malaga has offered us some gold to leave El Hacho behind. They come every twenty years or so and always return without a signature on their papers. You know why they value it so much?

They want the stone for their roads.

That's right. They want the stone for their roads, but do you know what is so special about Hacho's stone?

No.

Nothing. There's no shortage of mountains in the Serranía and they're all made of the same thing. They want our mountain for the reservoir that sits beside it. They need the water to cool the machines that will blast and claw at Hacho's sides and tear it down rock by rock. Can you imagine the scar this would leave behind?

Marie sighed heavily, ambushed by his brothers' passion.

Besides, Curro continued, raising his finger for emphasis.

To tear down that mountain would be to rip the heart from this village. The two are linked by a history that goes back to the Moors who built these streets and houses. I'm not educated enough to know the details but El Hacho is our version of the name they give to a mountain that watches over the people who live in its shadow, that protects them from those who would turn them out, and you don't have to go too far back to find another example. Jose Aguilar defended this town, and Benaoján, from Napoleon's troops with a crew of less than two hundred men and it was from Hacho's peak they saw them coming and prepared themselves. That mountain is the tallest in the Grazalema, the beacon. It has sat there for billions of years and we are just a speck beside it. Don't you understand this Marie? We don't own it, we are just its guardians, and for a very short time.

Our parents lie at the foot of that mountain. I'll not dig their bones from the earth for a house in Ronda and a car I have no use for. When I die, I'll lie down next to them and so should you.

Marie stared beyond him for a long time.

You forget one thing Francisco, he said eventually.

I've forgotten more than I know. There will be more than one thing.

Papa left it to us both. You alone cannot say what goes and what does not. I am entitled too.

Curro inclined his head and pursed his heavy lips.

I am not ignorant to this fact, he said. But be careful how you use that word. Entitlement. The inheritance carries a responsibility you have never understood, but I do not blame you for that. I have had a few days now to think this through and if you do not want the land to work you must be compensated somehow and if it is money that you want we can arrange for you to have it.

Marie's eyes sparkled like those of an old and patient vulture spying a wounded chamois finally fall on its knees and he leant in with his nose to sniff the deal.

I took a walk to Ronda yesterday to speak with Tomas Higuaín, Curro continued. His bank will forward a sum of money as a mortgage.

How will you repay it?

From the wages you would normally take. You can have the whole amount as a package now, or take a percentage of those wages every month until I am too old to work the olives. I'd rather you take the latter, but I sense you'll want the package.

I would.

I know it.

How much would it be?

Curro took an unhurried drink from his tumbler and fixed his brothers eyes with his own and didn't release them until the glass was empty. Then he dipped his hand into his own jacket pocket and retrieved a sheet of folded paper and unfurled it carefully and dropped it under his brothers' elbow. Marie took it warily and narrowed his eyes to read it and then set it down and bought his hand to his chin and stroked his upper lip with his finger and read the note again.

It's less than a quarter of the Hernandez offer, he said at length.

The Hernandez offer is a mirage in the desert, Curro replied sharply. As long as I have my strength that mountain will remain standing. I do not want to fight with you Marie. I want you to come back to work by my side and sweat and laugh with me, but I accept your determination to find your own way. This piece of paper is the only way for you to achieve it, believe me please.

Marie's expression conveyed enough resigned acceptance of the facts before him to forestall what remained of Curro's presentation so he returned the paper to his pocket and straightened the lapels of his coat. Marie reached for the bottle but it was empty of wine in his hand.

Where does this leave us? he asked.

As we were, I hope. I've drank just enough tonight for these old legs to find their way home but when I wake tomorrow you will be my brother still. My only request is that you go home to your wife and talk to her of the things we have discussed tonight. If you both feel the way you do now in a few days time I will go back to Señor Higuaín and arrange what needs to be done. Better still, we will both go together, but I want you to think Marie, deeply, that this is the thing you want. If you disinherit yourself from the land now, you can never have it back, and it may be worth more to you in time than the temporary riches dancing before your eyes. If you take the money from it, make sure you make the money work.

I will.

I pray you will.

You still pray Francisco?

Curro grinned slyly. Not by the bedside, he said. But in other ways I ask Him to smooth things over from time to time. He eased himself from the chair and cast his brother a final benevolent smile.

Come up and see me in a few days time and we'll share a cup of wine. Love to Almudena and the boys. He winked and turned and edged around the bodies at the bar and found Diego working the coffee pot and gripped his hand across the oak. He patted his hip pocket for his house keys and stepped unsteadily into the square for home.

# *Eleven*

The sun was angry upon the valley when he took his coffee to the terrace in the morning. He blew at the edges of the cup and pecked at it slowly and let it soothe the bludgeon of the wine his body was not practiced to endure.

He squinted through his fingers at the vault of blue spreading from Hacho's peak, across the red tiled roofs of the Montejaque village and down beyond the sharp teeth of the cordillera that receded into the horizon and in not one place could he find a note of imperfection. For just one wisp of hopeless cloud or a thin sheet of mist he wished and blew and drank some more.

He read the dull ache across his shoulders and up through his hips and for one mischievous second played with the thought of letting his body rest from work that day before grinning bitterly at the impossibility of such a thought. Despite his advice to Marie to sit on the deal they had made and reconsider it, he harboured no illusions that he would do so. This work was now his alone, a thought which dismayed and inspired him in equal measure.

He finished his coffee and nibbled at a side of bread and took his gloves and a puron of water and set out for the grove, stopping only to collect some of the pink flowers he used to decorate his parent's tomb and memory. He performed the graveside ritual quickly, almost carelessly, and whispered a few apologetic words to the stone as he stood and hoisted the satchel to his shoulder. Then he walked the length of the track he had already paved, dropped the satchel into the dust where it ended and set to work.

He grafted through the oven dry heat of the day, with neither haste nor pause, stopping only to drink from the puron. When five stone piles were forged he spat into his gloves and set them down, then drank and piled more stone and in this methodical, mechanical routine the path edged inexorably towards the reservoir at the perimeter of the grove.

Only when the sun had plunged beyond the valley and cast the grove in a slate blue shadow and the cuffs of his shirt were red with dust and the creases in his brow cut with the same ochre streaks did he think of returning home. When he entered the house his wife was wearing the worry of her love and she forced him to eat the stew despite his exhausted claim that he hadn't the strength to raise the spoon to his lips.

In the morning he beat both cockerel and sun out to the

terrace and repeated the travails of the previous day. A little coffee, an insufficient breakfast and hours of blistering work under a pitiless yellow orb. When he returned at sundown her concerns were close to hysterical but all he could offer her was the truth.

God will stop me if it's not meant to be done, he said and folded her hands in his and tucked a tress of hair behind her ear and dragged his sorry limbs upstairs to bed.

Despite the totality of his fatigue he was up before the birds when the morning came and laying stone before the sun leant around Hacho and evaporated what little mist the night had sent. He piled the stone and set it, then drank and piled some more.

Just after noon, when the sun was at its despicable worst and his collar wet with sweat and the tips of his gloves worn through to his bleeding fingers he walked to the nearest olive and lifted a flat stone the size of a melon. His muscles were shredded and the pain sawed into the pit of his neck but this particular stone carried absolutely no weight for it would be the last one he would have to lift. He dropped it into the space and cupped a handful of dust from beneath the same tree and fingered it into the cracks and blew the rest away and stood and rested his hand on the fence separating the grove from the reservoir edge and stared at the swampy puck of bile congregated at its centre. The pain wept through his body but now he embraced it with something akin to pleasure. He had earned it.

He whisked the hat from his head and fanned his face and

pulled it back on and collected his satchel and hobbled back down the grove along his creation. It was a long walk but that only gratified him the more. The longer he walked the greater the sense of accomplishment bloomed within him.

When he approached the house his brother was there, his gaunt frame leaning upon the open door of his car, a cigarette in his hand and his eyes downcast upon the gravel. Curro stopped five paces from him and waited until he met his eye. His tongue was swollen and heavy with dust and it clicked as he freed it from his mouth to speak.

So, are we going to Ronda?

Marie nodded meekly.

Curro felt the anguish burn his eyes shut as he passed his brother and mounted the terrace lip.

I'll wash and change he said, in a voice he did not recognise.

# *Twelve*

He threw the bedclothes from his chest and stroked his fingers through the damp hair upon it and wondered of the time. The shutters were down but spliced with a sharp orange bead that told the height of the sun already up. His wife was busy in the kitchen below and she was singing softly. He forced himself to his elbows and made to rise but his weary limbs forbade it so he lay and stared at the grey outlines of the beams and ran his fingers across his chest, where more hairs were silvery grey than were not.

He lay and devoted special thanks to providence that his olive grove was the meager size it was and no bigger for he could not have forced himself to work the track that day if it had remained unfinished. Soon the door creaked on its hinges and she entered carrying the warmth of her smile and a tray of eggs and coffee. She placed them on the table and sat on the bed beside him and crossed her hands in her lap.

You're wringing wet, she said. You feel a fever?

He shook his head and she leant in to him and felt his brow with the back of her palm.

You're sure?

I know it, he said and took her hand and kissed her fingers and held it on his chest.

You have worried me Curro, these past few days, she said. There was a fire in your eyes when you set off in the morning and nothing but exhaustion when you returned. Did you have to push yourself so hard?

The work would have stood a while, he said. God knows it's been standing for years already, but the only way I can think a thing through is to occupy my hands. It keeps me focused. The simpler the job, the more room to think, but if I stop completely my mind makes its own path and settles on something else. But I'm glad the job is done and we have Marie to thank for it really.

She frowned and straightened the pins in her hair and stood and pulled at the pillow beneath his head and pounded the shape into it and set it down beneath his back and now he was sitting against the wooden headboard. Then she transferred the tray into his lap and broke the eggs.

Curro, she murmured.

Yes.

I don't know how to feel about it.

He was about to blow the coffee but set it down and studied her with sly amusement.

It's only breakfast. What's to feel?

She sat back down and glowered at him. You'll feel this coffee in your lap if you make a game of me. I know you don't want to talk of it, and that's your choice, but you'll sit and listen to me.

You know it's not true, he said, the smile still playing at his lips. I've never even soaked a bowl of almonds without asking you what you think, but the sorry truth of it is, until Marie pulled up on my courtyard yesterday with that haunted look upon his face, I didn't think it would happen.

She frowned. I knew from the minute Almudena cornered me in the plaza and confessed his plans.

You're a better judge than me.

It's your optimism I love the most.

He shrugged and spooned the eggs into a roll of bread and closed it in his fist and tore the end off with his good teeth and chewed it slowly. At what point does optimism just become stupidity? he said.

She curved her shoulders and sighed. I think it could be a good thing for Marie but I doubt he understands why. And I worry for you, for the work of his that you must now do and how we will repay the debt. We've never had one before. But mostly I think about the two of you and the years you've spent together in the grove and wonder if he will come up here anymore. Will it change the way you feel for one another?

Curro sighed and thought a little.

Marie thinks he has let me down in some way and he feels a shame he shouldn't. He was never a willing worker and I told him enough times that he was born for other things and finally he started listening and did something about it. A man cannot feel truly free until his life is made from its own choosing. Marie has this now and it will bring him happiness for a while. My fear is that the choices are the wrong ones. For him.

You think he'll waste the money.

In my heart I do.

He drinks too much.

And now he has the means.

But for how long?

Who can tell? If he has inherited any of Papa's sense, and I'm sure there's just a little in him somewhere, he'll realise that money in itself is a false idol. People covet it without knowing why they do. For sure he'll buy some nice things with it and feel the flush of throwing some of it around but when the vanity of showing that you have it empties out and you realise that happiness isn't found of things you buy in shops you may be worse off than having never had it in the first place. God willing Marie will realise this before he tips it all down his throat and find a way to use it that brings him joy in what he does every day. But I've looked into his eyes and I don't believe he knows what that is. Just to get his hands on a pot of gold seems to be the limit of his imagination.

And what's the limit of yours? she asked.

He sipped at the lip of his cup and stared wistfully into the dark liquid.

I've never wanted more than the health to work my olives with the sun on my neck and the jabber of the choughs in my ears. Give me this and the chance to share a cup of wine on the terrace watching the stars with my love and I'll be content. There's riches right there.

She eyed him doubtfully. You don't worry for the debt though?

Of course, but don't forget we no longer have to split the take.

That's true.

I worry more for the rain.

I know it.

But if we have a bad year I'll sell a little parcel to Sergio. He always wants more room for his vines.

You'd sell some of Hacho?

He laughed at the irony.

Perhaps.

She shook her head irritably and collected the tray.

About time you were up, she said behind her as she left. And wash yourself. There's egg in your beard.

Curro hunted it down and sucked it off his finger. He swung his body from the bed and padded across the warm tiles in his shorts and on to the bathroom where he released the tap at the sink. The pressure was weak and as he waited for the bowl to fill, he squinted at his reflection in the mirror and fingered the creases that cut into his skin beneath the eyes and journeyed down his cheeks like tributaries to the larger ones framing his mouth. His face was old and weathered now, as old as his father's in his memory of him but the jaw was still strong and the hair line respectable and he felt he was ageing correctly in respect of his years and felt none of the self-pitying conceit some people use to lament nature's work upon them.

He washed and dressed and descended to the kitchen where he wrung another coffee from the pot and emptied a mound of almonds into his palm and crunched them as he took the force of the sun upon his cheeks on the terrace. It was high and heavy and he reproached himself for lying in his bed for such a time. The houses of the Montejaque village between the almond grove and the valley wall seemed to blister in the hot dry air. He turned and followed the outline of the crag that bordered the northern aspect of the village until it met the lower slopes of Hacho. The mountain shimmered brilliantly in the white hot light that pounded at its face and reflected onto the olives and desiccated the land around them.

Instinctively he thought to take a tour around the grove and check the swelling of the fruit but shuddered at the prospect of the slow death of his trees before his eyes and so he stayed on the terrace and nursed his coffee and picked the almonds from his teeth.

He thought of the Hernandez offer and wondered if he would overcome his pride and sell before he starved and balled his fist in anger on his knee and demanded to know why he, who asked for nothing more than the right to work a simple farm, should be deprived of the right to do so.

His wife broke the bitter clouds of his reverie with a hand upon his shoulder as she leant upon him to lower herself slowly to the terrace lip.

Give me your hand, she said and took his elbow and reached behind her and retrieved a soft grey mitten and slid it sweetly over his fingers. He cradled the gloved hand in his other and worked his thumb into the fabric and nodded his head and flexed the fingers within it.

It's good, he said. Tight at the wrist but there's room for the fingers to breathe. From the big buck I bagged last week?

She was beaming. The whole glove from just that buck.

That's good.

I've tanned three more this morning, she said. They're drying in the cellar.

He knotted his brow and released his sweating hand from the soft, velvet sheath. But what do we need them for? he asked. The ones you made the winter back are just working in now. How many hands do you think I have?

Now she was a show of cunning smiles, the corners of her delicate lips twitching as she shifted her hips on the terrace lip.

I'm going to sell them, she said.

Sell them to who?

There's a new place on the Calle Serrato. Señor Abellán will give me one hundred a pair and will take as many as I can make.

Curro stiffened on his seat, his face bruised with confusion. The Calle Serrato? In Ronda?

That's right.

When did you go to… how did you know to…?

While you were killing yourself on the track, she said. I took a bus and your own gloves and showed them at a few places. The owner of that big shop on the Bola, the one with the tall mahogany display stands, said he really liked them but he couldn't take any because he is tied into some contract with a factory in Antequera, so I walked around until I found Señor Abellán's place. Did I mention that he'll pay a hundred a pair?

I had no idea.

Why would you?

You don't mind the work?

I want to help.

He straightened his back and billowed his chest. You think this harvest will fail.

Don't let pride be the enemy of your belly Francisco, she said and squeezed his knee. You give every drop of yourself to this farm and if God does not reward you for it with a harvest worthy of your work, we'll still have a little coming in for flour and coffee.

He relaxed his rigid frame and leant across to kiss her and she angled her cheek to meet it. You're right, was all he said.

She took the glove and made to stand. So now you're busier than ever, she reminded him. With all the rabbits you are to catch for me.

I didn't think of that. How many will you need?

I can make two pairs a week, so you'd better bring me

six. They won't all be as big as this one. She patted the glove in her hand.

Curro contemplated the stand of almonds and the long thin leaves wrinkled by the drought and felt the bore of heat upon his crown and understood the even hand of fate. It might refuse to send him rain but what right did he have to curse it when it had sent her to him and in the final reckoning, he had come out well.

I'll do better than that, he said. Rain or not, this fruit will have to come in soon and then my hands are tied. I'd better make a start.

If you're not too tired.

One thing.

Yes.

Do we have to eat rabbit every night?

She shook her head. No, I'll swap the meat at Esmeralda's for some better cuts. It won't be much but that's alright.

Good. I'll start on the snares.

He flicked the coffee from the cup and watched it splash into the dust and handed her the cup as he stood and flexed the ache from his back. Then he mounted the terrace and walked across to the stable. It took him some time to find the sheet of leather and the wooden box of tools in the twilight of the stable and then he closed the door behind him and carried them behind the building to the shade.

He spread a blanket on the floor and placed the box upon it. Then he remembered that he'd need a piece of wood to lay beneath the leather whilst he cut the strips and scanned the yard for a suitable piece. There was a pile beside the figs which climbed the corner of the courtyard where the stable joined the house but when he got there the wood was mostly dry and brittle and bust apart too keenly in his hands. Then he recalled the plank he used for sowing seeds in springtime so as not to compact the earth he'd freshly tilled and went into the stable to retrieve it.

When he returned his shirt was sodden at the neck and fans of sweat were spreading beneath his arms and up across his back and he noticed there was a difference to the heat. The air was thick and cloying and the shadows on the courtyard had lost their definition and as he hinged his head towards the sky he found the ever present brilliance of the blue had been diluted by a shiny veil of misty cloud and the sun was tempered of its blinding wrath. If I didn't know better, he said to the plank, I'd say I smell some rain.

He took the wood across to the blanket and set it down beside the box and opened the lid and fingered amongst the tools. He found a leather sheath, dark and oiled and released the buckle and took a barbers razor with a pearlescent handle from it. He unhinged it and scraped his finger across the blade and nicked at a few of the hairs across his forearm and when they didn't come away without a second scrape he fingered through the box again and found a steel. Then he sat his back against the whitewash of the wall and ran the blade against the steel with slow and determined flicks of his wrist until he could see the fresh line of the blade emerge and then he tested it once more and found that it was good. All the while he whistled a simple pasodoble through his teeth and was content to be there.

He levered himself onto his knees and took the leather sheet and found a hammer with a rubber head from his box of tools and started to pummel the russet colored skin and as he did the sweat ran off his nose and dimples of it formed in darker circles on the surface of the skin.

When the sheet was flat and soft he laid it gently on the plank and reached behind him for the blade. Then he rested his weight on his palm to hold it firm and began to cut a line of leather no thicker than a stem of esparto grass and as he cut, he broke the melody of his tune with little grunts and held his grip and concentration until the narrow strip was free and coiled upon the blanket like a baby whip snake.

He sat back on his calves and took his breath and felt the heavy air drift round him in a rising breeze. The rattling din of the insects amongst the grasses was dying to a murmur and as he craned his neck to Hacho's peak he saw a sky devoid of birds. Not even the griffon vultures, so fond of the thermals that build off the valley and rise up Hacho's belly and twist away over the Grazalema, minded to be flying through air so thick and rank you could cup a pool of it in your hand and watch it seep between your fingers.

Curro felt a low and slender frisson lace his stomach and ride up through his chest. By some visceral barometer only farmers know he felt the pressure of the air had dropped, but he dared not chase the belief it would bring the rain because he could not bear it if his hopes were to be empty yet again. So he rocked upon his knees and took the blade and set to cut the leather.

Whilst he worked he occupied his mind with the question of the alcohol he would need to soften the snares when they were cut and if he had enough left over from the time before and if he could remember where the thing was stowed. He went into the stable and used a book of matches to light the room, which had grown much darker, and found a long necked ceramic bottle stoppered with a wooden bung. When he lifted it from the shelf he knew by the weight he'd have enough to work the snares and he took it with a shallow bowl and dusty rag from the stable.

Without haste or pause Curro worked and soon had cut twenty cords of leather from the sheet of skin which was now reduced to half its former size. He leant back against the wall and wiped around his neck and ears with the cuff of his shirt and thumbed the wooden stopper from the jar and poured the colorless spirit into the bowl. Then he soaked the rag. When it was good and full he squeezed it over the bowl and folded it in his palm and took a reed of leather and pulled it slowly through the cloth.

Each cord required five journeys through the sodden rag and he made each one slowly and the spirit began to eat into the grazes on his knuckles and make them nip and sting like the tiny lances of mosquito bites.

When he placed the final cord onto the plank to dry he noticed that no shadow lay on the ground around him so he cast his eyes towards the sky and there was nothing but a solid sheet of speckled grey stretched across the heavens. The wind was chasing spools of dust into the corners of the courtyard where they pooled in graceful coils of golden brown and broke up in the agitated thrashing of the air and formed again in another place. He wiped his hands on the blanket and poured the liquid from the bowl into the ceramic jar. As he took to his cramped and unsure legs he heard a hollow, baritone growl echo in the sky towards the east.

He held his breath and raised a solitary eyebrow. Then it came again, but in a conjoined series of rolling groans, like the celestial plucking of a cello's lowest note and his breath began to tremor. He staggered backwards across the yard, his head hinged skyward and the wind flapping the collar of his shirt against his neck and as he came up from beneath the protection of the stable towards the kitchen garden he saw the horizon beyond the eastern valley invaded by great shapeless towers of purple-black thunder heads streaked upon their hulls with sulphuric yellow light. They heaved across the sky in frothing anger and the groaning of the thunder began to clap in peals of shocking weight.

To his left a stand of dying sweetcorn stalks rattled their brittle leaves into the tearing wind and to his right he saw the squares of light flash in the windows of the houses of the Montejaque village and then extinguish as the shutters came across. The kitchen door snapped open and his wife was on the terrace with her apron dancing on her hips and her hands across her mouth. She gaped at the enveloping flood of darkness surging towards her and turned to find him and when she did a jagged charge of molten light crackled beyond the valley wall and flashed against the house.

She cupped her hands to shout to him above the wind and crashing thunder but he was running through the grove and up amongst the boulders of the slope of Hacho's base and then scrambling further, higher up onto the scree and sending fragments of it down in channels from his boots. Finally he made the little cave and there he turned and leant against the maw of the opening, screeching for breath with his pulse hammering in his ears.

Now he had a higher view above the valley wall and he watched the shifting leviathans of purple and anthracite twisting together and bellowing their rage, charged with erratic flares of incandescent white within the cloud like grapeshot issuing through the mist of some terrible military reckoning.

Curro stood and sucked at his tongue to find some spit. As he drew enough to swallow, an orb of rain the size of a pipit's egg exploded on the tip of his nose and sprayed fine droplets across his beard.

# *Thirteen*

Curro leant his weight upon the handle of the mop and listened to it filter in the pail. Then he swiped it against the bottom of the door and stood and watched the water seep indefatigably back through. The rain like grit hurled against the shutters by some angry hand. And still it came.

I should have made a sandbag, he said.

Who could have guessed at this? she replied.

Still.

Come and finish your coffee.

It's the coffee that makes me agitated. I've done nothing but drink for three days now.

Sit then. You'll no more stop that water than turn a cock into a hen. Let it come a while and save yourself some work.

He grumbled in his throat and leant the mop against the rim of the pail and paced a circle on the kitchen floor and then parked himself against the dormant stove.

Is it too much to ask? he said.

What?

For a little balance.

You asked me that already. I didn't know the first time.

Months without a drop and now this, he said and shook his head and sucked at his thumb nail. Papa used to tell me that a Spanish horse can only stand or dance, and in them both it has no equal. I used to think he was talking about horses.

It makes us what we are.

He tore at the nail with his teeth and spat the paring into the sink.

She looked at him malevolently and said, Curro, I swear by San Tiago himself that if you do not find a better way to be until this passes we shall come together in a manner you will not like.

He steepled his brow at her and filed the nail edge against his teeth, knowing better than to talk.

If you want something to do you can help me cut this skin, she said and gestured at the table with the scissors in her hand.

You don't need the help to do it though.

But I need the peace from your shuffling to and fro. Sit or leave.

I could do a round of the traps.

You know they won't take in this rain but I won't tell you not to.

They might have.

Go then.

He had his palms against the stove rail and chewed at the inside corner of his mouth in thought. The electric element fizzed dully in the lamp above his head and the crisp nip of the scissors coming together through the skin made a harmony with the relentless rattle of the rain against the door and shutters. He drummed his fingers on the rail and then pushed himself upright.

I'll go, he said. This is making me crazy.

She sighed in agreement.

He passed her at the table on his way to the pantry door and stepped inside. He took the oilskin from a hook and reached into the corner for his rubber boots and carried them all into the kitchen and placed them on the floor beside the wooden chair and sat and eased a foot inside but paused as it reached the ankle and removed it. He folded the cuffs of his trousers into each sock and shod himself properly and stood and whisked the oilskin around his shoulders, lifting green and mouldy odours from it. Then he remembered his trapping satchel and returned to the pantry but could not find it there.

It's on the shelf under the sink, she said when asked.

I left it there? he said doubtfully

No, you left it lying around. I put it there.

He strode to the sink and knelt and slid the chequered curtain on its cord and groped at his satchel and threw his arm through the leather strap and pulled it around his head. Then he walked to the door and cowled himself in the cavernous hood of the oilskin and stamped his boots dramatically and turned to her in expectation of a benediction for some noble and dangerous adventure and when none came he shrugged and hefted the latch.

He closed the door behind him upon her sharp advice to do so faster and walked to the lip of the terrace and arched his head under the oilskin hood to see the world about him. The rain bit at his cheeks but was not cold. Three days of ceaseless waterstorm had transformed the palette of the land to a degree he could not have supposed during the drought, reducing the pink tinged clay of the unpaved tracks to a heavy taupe and the lively green spray of the olive leaves to a denser stagnation of the same colour. They were slick with water and shivering under the weight as each leaf tried to shrug itself free of an unyielding torrent. The homogonous grey of the sky stretched unchanging beyond the cordillera to the coast and the Montejaque village sat damp and smoking before it.

He heard the rattle of the mop and pail behind the door and allowed himself a smile and retracted his head within his shoulders and dropped down off the terrace in the direction of the grove. He made the paved section bisecting the plot in little hops to avoid the rutted pools and tested the stones with heavy steps of his boots, the wind whipped tassels of the olive branches swirling around him. Content that the rain had not loosened the foundation of the track he stepped to a tree leaving a trail of shapeless prints that quickly filled with water and collapsed within themselves.

He plucked a handful of fruit. It was colouring well now and had a healthy waxen sheen and the flesh had a better resistance in his mouth when he rolled one on his tongue and chewed it slowly. He spat it into the mud and raised his head to Hacho's peak.

Molested by the sheets of swirling mist and rain he continued through the grove to meet the road. He took great care climbing the wall that ran between them, the stones now slick where the rain had glossed the lichen and he headed north upon the road between rivulets of water which bubbled up from the shallow gutters and eddied into the cracks in the tarmac and then washed on.

He hadn't made fifty yards when he saw the back of a hunched oilskin wedged into a thick row of vines in the plot to his right. The figure emerged with a handful of fruiting canes and a sodden straw hat, erupting at patches in the crown and dripping a skirt of water across his shoulders. He threw the canes to the ground and snipped with spontaneous violence at something he'd missed in the leaf canopy.

Curro whistled low and clear. The man turned slowly and took a pipe from between his teeth and reset it there and lifted the flap of a pocket in the oilskin, lacquered black by the rain, and stowed the shears and walked towards the wall where Curro lifted a foot to a foundation stone and leaned upon his knee.

Francisco, the man said.

Sergio.

How is it?

Wet.

God's truth. He took the pipe and pointed it at Curro's grove. You bringing them in?

Curro shook his head. Another week at least, he said. I'll let them have a good drink and when it blows on we'll see about it.

The wireless couldn't say when it might be.

Is that so? I thought this would be the tail end of it now.

The wireless couldn't say. Do you have a match?

Not here with me. You'll not light that with a gas torch though.

Sergio dropped an eye into the briar and tamped it with his thumb. Could be right, he said.

How's your own? Curro asked, adjusting the hood of his coat and wiping the rain from his forehead with a curved finger. I'm surprised to see you out in this.

I'm just opening them up a little, so the wind can get at them. They're coming well now mind, but if the water sits on them for too long they might start to moulder. It's been known.

How do they fare up here usually?

What's usual?

When the weather isn't so up and down?

The altitudes a blessing. Keeps them cooler of a night than down off the Serranía which slows them down a bit.

And this affects the wine?

For sure. More time to develop their flavour means better flavour. Not that it helps me any. The collective pays all the same on weight. If I had the ways to brew and bottle it myself I could turn out a decent vintage. Better than the swill that comes out of the collective.

Why don't you?

Sergio regarded him frankly. You know what a bit of oak barrel costs and how many I'd need to start up?

I've never thought on it.

More than the collective pays me for the whole of this lot in spring and that just about lasts me to the next one.

Never considered a loan?

Sergio gnashed on the stem of his pipe sourly and focused one eye on Curro. I've never owed as much as a peseta in this world and I'm too old to start now, he said. First bad harvest and they'd take the lot away from me.

I feel the same way, said Curro. I wouldn't wish you to do it.

Why are you so interested?

I'm just talking. A man down in Montejaque asked me why I didn't grub up the grove and plant it with vines when the sun was baking the hell out of it and the wind was picking at the roots.

It picks at vine roots just as easily.

I suppose it does.

I'll let you have a little piece of advice Curro, he said, removing the hat and smoothing back the reedy streaks of hair across his mottled crown. And you can use it however you like.

Go on.

You inherited that patch from your own as I did this one from mine.

That's right.

So we didn't have a choice about what was in it when it came to be ours.

That's about the length of it.

So all you have to do when you turn in at night is curse your luck and the weather. If you go changing things and it all goes to shit around you, then you've got your stupidity to lie considering, and that'll keep a man awake a damn sight longer.

Curro smiled greatly and lifted his foot from the stone and tapped at it with his toe. That's some good advice.

Sergio replaced the hat. Use it, it's free.

I will. Take care now.

Where are you going in this?

I thought I'd check the traps. Get out from under Carmen's feet.

Rabbits? They'll not take in this rain.

I know it.

You'll not be disappointed then.

No. Take care now.

Come again Curro, he said and turned back upon his vines, his hand already in the pocket for the shears.

Curro turned on the road and pulled the hood around his ears, the rain drumming woodenly upon it. He leant on his thighs and turned upon a car revving behind him. He stepped to the gutter to let it pass and when it did he tried to recognise the driver but the windows were fogged. The wind reared up through the valley and cast the rain in horizontal rods around him yet on he continued, his head bowed penitentially under its curse.

He walked the rising loop of the road until the reservoir appeared to his left and the plateau stretched across the scrub and cork oak towards the peaks of the Grazalema range, capped by the belly of the clouds and he stood and regarded the still grey water, higher now than he'd seen it since winter. A solitary bird skated the surface and climbed and disappeared into the rock face.

He passed the junction of the service road that twisted down towards the engineering buildings at the water's edge until the cutting of a track emerged amongst the cork trees. He walked with arms high along the central spine of the track, grooved on either side by the wheels of the cork carts, the mud sucking at his boots and releasing each step with unctuous reluctance until he found a lesser artery through the brush and stooped under a rain blackened branch to ford it. The footing became surer but the fingers of wet brush swiped at his oilskin as he twisted through.

He made a small clearing and sat on his calves and parted the knives of grass around a leather chord, wet and empty. He reset the snare and collected the red cloth marker that had fallen in the deluge and retied it to a sapling above the trap.

His round took him past four more empty traps which he reapplied with care into the runs where rabbits might dare to tread and the cold spread into his fingers and wrists which he flexed and rubbed and wondered what he was achieving there alone and exposed. He briefly considered turning back but realised that the path ahead was the shorter route to home.

He stepped upon a flat bluff of limestone, with juvenile agave set into the sink holes and dropped off the other side onto a grassy plate framed with the trunks of cork oak and caught a red marker bobbing gently on its mark. Beneath it the grass thrashed and heaved between two rocks, each no bigger than the wheel of a car and as he drew upon it the lynx lifted its head and flattened its spine and then writhed in frantic spasms of fear.

He bent low and redrew his steps and the animal contorted some more and then rent the clearing with a diabolic squeal, and fixed him with its beautiful, murderous eyes and growled low and flat unto him. He retreated to the bluff and lowered himself upon the lip of it and laid his hands upon his knees. The lynx bucked again and flung itself back in a succession of wretched movements and was pinioned each time by the snare around its paw which tightened with every frenzied effort. It coiled in the grass and issued its sibilant mew.

Now you know how the rabbit feels, said Curro but not maliciously and now his only thoughts were spent on how to free it.

The snare was an old one, not part of the batch he'd recently made and one he'd long since disregarded. He squinted through the rain to find the anchor point and saw that it was cast around the boulders themselves and wondered how it hadn't snapped upon the torrid exertions of the cat and congratulated his ability to set a good snare.

He opened his satchel and took out his knife and hinged it back until the lock clicked and he weighed it in his palm. Then he stood and moved, low and sure in an arc around the circumference of the clearing until he was just a pace from the boulder. The lynx erupted in a whirl of fur and hateful wails and pressed itself to the grass and then reared and flashed its free paw, crowned with ivory picks and twisted its head and came again, but Curro knew it couldn't reach him. He lay in the grass, the boulder between him and the cat and ground the knife against the leather chord held taut against the rock and as it cut there was a whisking sound and then a crash of foliage and nothing but the rain drumming on the leaves.

# *Fourteen*

He hoisted the sandbag upon his shoulder and grimaced at the creak in his knee and stood a moment and worked the joint and then scuttled across the stable under the weight of the sack. As he pushed open the door the sun hit him in a florescent flash and he blinked and retreated back to the shadows and then re-emerged into the heat of it like a wary snail from its shell. The brooding hulls of blackened cloud collided and foamed around the bright aperture of light and then it was gone and he was cast back into ominous dark.

He scanned the horizon above the valley wall for further breaks of hope but none appeared amongst the charcoal weave of cloud and by the time he crossed the terrace and dropped the sandbag against the heap before the kitchen door the rain was pattering once more upon the oilskin on his back. He leant his weight on the structure and hammered the edge of his fist at the corners where each bag met to force the joins. Then he stood and thumbed the latch and pushed the door and stepped over the barricade into the kitchen.

As the door clicked shut the rain reared upon it and he unbuttoned the oilskin and walked to the pantry and laid it on a hook and knelt to free his boots and then padded across the kitchen tiles and rustled some coffee from the pot. He took it to the table and sat and blew gently at the rim and watched the gap between the tiled floor and kitchen door, lifting his toes as he drank.

He sat staring at that black slit, long after the coffee was gone. The rain hurled itself relentlessly against the door but the water did not penetrate through. When his wife descended the stairs in her clogs, he broke his trance and fixed her with a determined look.

It's time to bring them in, he said.

# *Fifteen*

He shaved himself closely and patted his face dry with a cloth which he folded neatly upon the rail. Returning to the bedroom he twisted the window latch and opened the pane and pushed at the wooden shutter, greasy under his palm and green around the edges. A veil of drizzle covered the valley and the sky was an unblemished, monotonous grey mirror of the stewing Montejaque village beneath it. At the toe of the village, a great lake had formed to cover the road that traverses the valley and climbs its eastern slopes in switchbacks on its way to Ronda and from its centre jutted the yellow roof of a car, the last to attempt the crossing. A month had passed since then.

He closed the window and fastened the latch and took a shirt from the back of the chair and slipped his shoulders through it. He was buttoning the front when he came upon a kitchen ready in the smell of bacon. Eggs were hacking in the pan and the bread lay sliced on the board upon the table. His wife was sifting flour into a glass bowl and when she heard him scrape the chair leg across the tiles to sit, she turned and smiled and poured the coffee.

How many eggs? she said.

How many do we have?

Two.

In all?

She nodded.

Have you eaten? he asked.

No.

Then one apiece.

I'll not need them.

No?

No.

She took a plate from the rack and wiped it with her apron and took the pan off the heat and slid the eggs onto the plate and then knelt and opened the stove door and collected another fold of apron to handle the tray inside. She placed it on the range and picked at the bacon with twitching pecks of her fingertips and dropped each piece onto the plate and carried it to the table. She set it down before him and arranged some bread on the lip of the plate, making sure not to break the yolks and then sat down in another chair and regarded the work.

Eat, she said.

Are you fattening me for a sale? he said, casting wary glances at the glistening heap.

If you're serious about bringing the fruit in, she said, and I know that you are, you'll need it. I lay thinking on it last night. It normally takes four days to do it all, but that's with the sun on your back and Marie at your side, so maybe a week on your own, maybe more. We've enough bacon for then, but I'll have to go see Concha for the eggs.

How are we for money?

I'll take some but I've a pair of gloves she might be glad to trade. Her husband spends a lot of time on the plateau in the winter.

Those gloves are worth more than a box of eggs.

She might have cheese and coffee as well, if the weather hasn't stopped the delivery.

The reservoir road is still open.

Good. Are you waiting for an invitation? Eat.

He rotated the plate a quarter turn and took the knife and split a yolk and dabbed at it with some bread and chewed slowly. She twisted a tongue of hair around her finger and let him eat.

When he finished he smothered a belch and slurped at his coffee, tepid and sweet, and breathed expansively and hooked an arm behind the chair.

You don't want to do it, do you? she said softly.

I could just as easily not. It's as well I haven't a choice.

You can't wait for the rain to break?

Who knows when it will? They've been ready for a week now.

It has to break some time.

In another week they'll have gone over and who's to say that it'll stop by then. It's already beyond anything anybody has ever known.

I know.

What can you do?

She shrugged. At least it's not in the house. Almudena's cousin lives up in the barrio, in Ronda. The road down from the campo is a river now, black with mud and it's washed straight through the street and cleared out the ground floor of the house. The furniture they couldn't save is just floating in it. Her mother sick in bed too.

You've seen Almudena? he asked.

I called in to see the boys.

How are they?

Restless.

And Marie?

He wasn't there but she frowned when I asked of him. He has a new car.

Is he turning his hand?

She didn't say.

Curro pushed himself clear of the table and frisked the breadcrumbs from his shirt.

Francisco?

Yes.

You should see him.

I'll go when the olives are in.

The longer you leave it though.

I know, he said abruptly and turned to the pantry door.

He leaned inside to reach his boots and oilskin and the crockery rattled behind him as she cleared it from the table.

He stamped his feet into the boots and whisked the coat around him and pushed his fingers through his hair and was out, over the sandbag rampart and onto the terrace where red water covered the toes of his boots and he sloshed through it on his way to the stable.

Inside he groped at a bundle of netting and took it out across the courtyard to the stable. He dropped it at the door and went inside and whisked a canvas cover from a machine that lay in the corner. It had a diesel motor at one end, similar in size to that of a large chainsaw which was attached to a long metal pole. The end of the pole flared into a circular ring, perpendicular to the pole itself and a leather strap fastened to the pole and to the rear of the motor.

He twisted a cap at the top of the motor and held it up to what light crept through the tiny, barred window and peered furtively into the fuel tank.

Enough to get me going, he said.

He reached onto a shelf and took a long, thin stick and flexed it with both hands to near breaking point. Then he grabbed the pole of the motor and carried it out of the stable where he placed it by the parcel of netting. He untangled four pieces of net from the bundle and kicked the remainder into the stable and closed the door and lifted the motor again and heaved a great sigh of foreboding and walked up the track to the grove, his footprints disappearing quickly behind him in the shifting mud.

He made the paved track which bisected the grove and cast around for a starting point amongst the trees and settled for a large split-trunked olive on the Hacho side which had never let him down. Leaving the motor on the path he took the nets to the base of the tree and spread them underneath the branches, which bowed heavily to the floor under the weight of fruit and rain, until the ground beneath the tree was covered in netting. The mud sucked at his boot heels as he spread the nets and he knew they'd blister his skin raw before the day was through.

He stood and wiped the water from his cheeks and brow and looked at the sky and saw it darken further over the valley wall to the east and he could only know the position of the sun behind the great morass of cloud from knowledge alone. The rain came greater still and washed on his neck and ran coldly down his spine.

He walked to the motor and lifted it slightly and twisted a switch at the base and laid it back down and put his foot on the pole. Then he reached for the rubber starter and took a breath which he held tight and pulled at the handle with the sum of his strength. The motor kicked and coughed but didn't turn. He yanked at the starter again and then again until it caught and a pall of blue smoke vaporised him briefly and the thing groaned and rattled on the paved track. He held the pole tightly, surprised as he always was at harvest time of its weight, and threw the leather strap across his shoulder and lifted it to his waist and staggered with it to the tree. It vibrated madly in his hands and the mud, loose and slick beneath his feet doubled the effort of the task.

With great concentration he planted the circular ring against the olive trunk just beneath the fork and leaned his full weight upon it. The tree began to dance and immediately the fruit started to fall, cascading to the net in a shower of black orbs that pattered onto the soft ground. The pole was slippery under his grasp and he groaned as his feet slathered around and still he leant into the motor until the exertion burnt in his forearms and thighs. He released the ring from the trunk and dipped his head about to see the effect and gritted his teeth and leant into it again. The tree vibrated hysterically around him but the remaining fruit was obdurately resistant to the machine's persuasion and shook on their stalks but wouldn't relinquish their grip.

He removed the ring from the trunk and fingered the switch to kill the motor and returned it to the paved track in slow, glissading steps. Massaging his fingers into the base of his spine he cast his face skyward and let the rain dapple his hot brow. To the east the din of brewing thunder. He walked back to the olive and took the stick from the net and whipped the air about him in two short bursts and then began to thrash at the branches. Shreds of leaves and stalk came spiraling down with the stubborn fruit and formed a carpet of ravaged foliage upon the raft of pebbly black olives.

When he had removed all of the fruit he could reach, he inched closer to the base of the trunk, unbuttoned his oilskin and slotted the stick into his belt. Then he took a firm hold of a branch at eye level with both hands, hoisted his mud clogged boot to the fork and with no little effort, hauled himself into the canopy. Twice his boot skated from the fork until he had the confidence to lean his weight upon it and continue his work. He beat the tree with more anger than skill and for longer than he ought to and for the first time in over a month, he admitted to himself the regret he felt at his brother's absence.

He descended carefully and gathered the outlaw fruit that had fallen beyond the perimeter of the nets and tossed them back into the mass. He stooped to finger the edges of a net to draw it up when he remembered he'd forgotten the cart and winced and stood and trudged his way back through the grove under a darkening mood. He found the cart under a heap of sacking in the corner of the stable and trailed it back through the mud to the track where he laid it on its shafts next to the motor.

As he returned to the nets his right boot slipped beneath him and he fell to his knees and the red slush of earth swallowed his hands as he forced himself upright and he cursed and spat with recriminating bile at all the forces arrayed against him. He wiped his hands against the oilskin and stepped foal-like to the nets and picked at the larger shards of leaf and stalk. He collected the first net at the edges and tipped the fruit into the centre until it bowed into a sack and when it was centered he twisted the netting into his fist and hauled it over a shoulder and carried it to the cart and released the olives into it. The sound of the fruit dashing into the wooden cart was normally a pleasant augury to him but now it was not. It only served to remind him of the commission afore him. He repeated the maneuver three more times and spread the fruit evenly in the cart and straightened his back and scanned the grove.

That's one, he said.

By the time he wearily lifted a boot onto the terrace lip the evening had gathered around him in a black swathe. He fumbled the door latch open and blinked at the soft yellow light and stepped across the sandbags and stood on the brown tiled floor like some mud-blown apparition of primordial life. His wife bought her hand to her mouth briefly and swallowed and pointed to the table.

Sit and I'll warm your food, she said.

He released the buttons of his oilskin and kicked off his earth caked boots and let it all fall into a grisly heap on the tiles and lowered his head and clambered up the stairs to his bed.

# *Sixteen*

For three more days he grafted in the sodden waste of the grove until by some time on the fourth he had collected all of the fruit that bore from the trees on the Hacho side of the track and now he was a shadow of the man that set out to win the harvest. His labour had slowed with every passing hour, but the rain did not relent its pitiless drum and now it ran in grey-red scars down Hacho's belly and pooled deep in clefts and hollows between the trees. He was a man accustomed by life to working hard the lines of the land but the candle of light which guided him through the toughest of times was dimming close to the taper.

He trailed the cart through the mud to the track as though he were making the Stations of the Cross and collapsed upon it in a ball of mud and crumpled oilskin, flecked with the green shrapnel of olive leaves.

Halfway, he said to the wrinkled fingers in his lap. He

imagined a doubling of the grief his body reported and actually laughed and knew he wouldn't get that far. He sat immobile on the cart, the rain slipping off his nose in an itchy torment he did not scratch. When no constructive thought befell him in that time he felt his body move from the cart and retrieve the nets and take them to the nearest tree and spread them around its base and return to the track for the motor like the automaton he had become.

The floor of the grove was now water itself, and so it splashed freely around his ankles as he moved them painfully to the olive. He leant the motor against the tree and pulled at the starter handle with slow repeated tugs until eventually it caught and rattled and smoked. He drew the harness across curved shoulders and planted the ring into the trunk and rested his weight into the tree and set his teeth tight in his jaw and pushed.

The fruit fell sporadically and he felt that the tree was shaking him of all the strength that remained unto him. He stepped back to find a better spot and when he rejoined the vibrating ring it dug into the bark and splintered it and skimmed around the trunk and the weight of the motor pulled him forward off his toes and down into the watery grime. He landed in a splash of panic and diesel smoke and the thing writhed madly in his hands and he gulped at mouths of gritty water as he twisted his body out from the harness. He pushed himself away and tried to stand but only slipped in the morass and careered backwards in another flailing splash. He lay, half dazed, half floating and heard the motor whine and finally putter to its death and above him there was a marble grey sky perfect in its indifference to his plight.

He rolled to his hands and knees and sat on his calves and balled his fists and trembled with a putrescent rage swelling somewhere deep and foreign within him into a force he couldn't master. It exited his being in a screech that shook the birds from their hidden perches and scattered them across the grove and upwards towards El Hacho in erratic black clouds.

YOU! he roared at the mountain, his fist raised high and quivering in wretched anger, his eyes red wells of pain.

What do you want of me? What do you *want* of me? Have I not loved you? Have I not *protected* you when they wanted to pull you down? Was it not enough for you, you stinking shit of rock to send me something better than this for my loyalty? Do I not deserve your love, have I not *earned* enough of your affection for you to save me from this mud? Was it not enough to bake my brains and wring every drop of sweat that now you have to drown me and my land, *your land*, in this never ending flood!

*Answer me!* he bawled, his arms aloft, the words like broken glass in his throat.

El Hacho echoed his cry across the valley and pressed its ancient weight upon him. He plunged his head into his hands and wept.

As he whimpered softly he felt a warmth spread across his neck and back and when he lifted his head the sun was glinting in white blades on the water that stood in the grove and decorating the trees in delicate motes of light.

Across the track the bull stood between two olives and heaved its great chest and bored its eyes into him and didn't blink or move. Its dense black hide, slick like oil, rippled and shivered in silver-blue streaks in the sun. They stared at each other for an eternity until the bull, provoked by no exterior force that Curro could observe, lifted its hooves and disappeared back through the grove.

Curro pushed himself afoot, picked the stick from the net and began to beat the fruit from the tree.

# *Acknowledgments*

This book would never have been conceived had I not been privileged to spend time living in the Sierra de Grazalema and the Serranía de Ronda for a short period of my life. My love and gratitude for the wonderfully open-hearted people who inhabit those mountains is reflected on every page.

I would like to extend my grateful thanks to Epoque Press for all of their expertise and patience in editing the original work and for enabling this story to be realised.